MELBA THE MUMMY

MELBA THE MUMMY

Ivy Ruckman

A YEARLING BOOK

Published by
Dell Publishing
a division of
Bantam Doubleday Dell Publishing Group, Inc.
666 Fifth Avenue
New York, New York 10103

The trademark Yearling® is registered in the U.S. Patent and Trademark Office.

The trademark Dell® is registered in the U.S. Patent and Trademark Office.

ISBN: 0-440-40437-1

Printed in the United States of America

April 1991

10 9 8 7 6 5 4 3 2 1

OPM

In Memory of Geoff
With special thanks to Libby Ellis and Holly Flora,
who care about the Earth

CONTENTS

1

In the Shopping Mall

What's the fun of being a genius if you never get invited to parties? Melba frowned and captured the last oat-flake against the side of her cereal bowl. There were six summer birthdays among her classmates at Morton Elementary. She'd checked. But Samuel Dexter, a friend since kindergarten, was the only one to invite her.

Under the kitchen table, Boots's tail thump-thump-thumped against the floor as he threw all his basset hound energy into begging. Melba tossed him a bite of toast. *Smack!* went his jaws with Gotcha Gator precision.

"Dad, let's go, I'm finished," she shouted in the direction of the computer den.

She carried her dishes to the sink, thinking about

last spring's Science Fair when she'd actually been popular. She'd been so certain then that kids would start liking her better.

Most of the time, of course, she loved being a genius. She grinned, remembering her fantastic breakthrough last year. It had been plenty scary, being on the Animals' Planet where Uprights were considered strays, but she'd learned so much. In her everyday life on Earth, however, being the class "brain" was definitely a handicap. Kids treated you funny. They expected you to be different.

Melba sighed and pushed up her glasses. She didn't feel different. With a new school year about to begin, she yearned to be an ordinary kid—one who got B's and C's on her report card and, occasionally, a "needs improvement" note from a teacher.

An hour later Melba and her dad walked into the crowded shopping mall, laughing and swinging hands. Her dad whistled snatches from "Come, Shop with Me," a waltz tune from his time, as he put it.

Melba turned to check their reflection in Myers Shoe Shop. Her father wasn't TV-tall-and-handsome, but he looked extra nice today. She liked his smiley eyes, the rim of hair that poufed out over his ears, even the way he whistled through his teeth.

"No daughter of mine is going to a birthday party

in holey jeans," he'd said the day her one-and-only invitation came in the mail.

Melba wouldn't have cared about the jeans. Not having a mother meant she ordered most of her clothes from catalogs, anyway, but a shopping trip sounded like fun.

"Afterward," he'd promised, "we'll have lunch in the Tiffin Room."

At the time Melba had rolled her eyes. The Tiffin Room didn't serve tacos, fries, or shakes. It was a place where older ladies met for tea and little sandwiches, where *his* mother had taken him.

"May I help you?" a pencil-thin saleslady asked a minute later when they walked into Young Fashions.

"Ummm, yes," her father answered. "My daughter is going to a birthday party."

"Lucky girl!" said the lady, beaming at Melba. "Whose party is it?"

Melba smiled back. "Samuel Dexter's. Do you know him?"

"No, I'm sorry to say. But it makes a difference what kind of party you're going to. As to what you'll wear, that is. So we'll rule out the cotillion dress . . . seeing that it's a boy's party."

Melba glanced up at her dad, whose tie had twisted off center, making him look like a baffled tourist. If she didn't know what a cotillion dress was, her engineer father certainly wouldn't.

They followed the lady's clickety heels to a circular rack.

Red nails flashing, she pulled out one, two, three Esprit coordinates and hooked them over the other clothes. There was a cropped shirt in bright pink—the great logo right there on the chest—and a tiger-striped skirt in the new short length.

"Oooh," Melba murmured, stroking the shiny fabrics.

"Complete your outfit with a denim jacket . . . one that just begs to have its sleeves turned up.

"Or"—the saleslady led them farther into the store—"we have these sweet new dresses that just arrived. Paisleys, with lacy collars. Do you like to be at the forefront of fashion, young lady?" She got right down to peer in Melba's face.

Melba shrugged, not knowing what to say.

Her father spoke up. "I'm in favor of a dress. Her aunt—my sister," he explained, "always dresses her daughters to the nines."

Nines! Astrocat's call number was nine. Astrocat . . . who had landed in her own backyard, silver space suit and all, the day she'd discovered Synergesis. She could see him shaking his fuzzy head. She could hear him scolding, "Now you've done it! How can I get on with my spying with you grounding me like this?"

"Melba?"

She jumped.

"Are you with us?" Her father cleared his throat. "We need an opinion."

Melba blinked. "What *I* need"—she was looking at the dresses but still seeing her dear friend, Astrocat—"is some new jeans, girls' size ten."

"Ah, yes!" the lady agreed, realizing the dresses were getting nowhere. "And with a few Guess tops to go with them—right, dear?"

Melba turned around in time to see her dad snatching up price tags, staring first at one, then another. By the time he caught up with them, he looked as if he were getting the flu.

Two hours later they left the store carrying five packages between them.

The big box contained a party dress that reminded her dad of one his sister had worn. "Of course," the saleslady was quick to point out, "your daughter definitely needs a hair bow with a dress like that."

"She does?" her father had squeaked.

"Oh, definitely. You want her to look like everyone else, I'm sure."

Melba smiled gratefully.

So they'd bought an enormous yellow bow to help tame Melba's every-which-way yellow hair. Four other bags contained jeans and T-shirts, socks, underwear, the tiger skirt, and the studded denim jacket whose sleeves were just dying to be rolled up.

Her father's face had definitely gone pink writing the check.

He was still muttering "Thirty dollars a T-shirt!" over the gooseberry pie he ordered later in the Tiffin Room.

2

Birthday Party Blues

The Saturday before school started, the day of Samuel's party, Melba stood "dressed to the nines" in front of her bedroom mirror.

"I don't know," she said, turning both ways to peer at herself. The belt was too tight and the nylons were hot, but she did look more like her cousin. Her father, who'd been acting as if *he* were going to the party, had put the bow in her hair fourteen different ways before he gave up and shouted, "You do it!"

Melba giggled. Her very own father, who could figure the stress ratios for steel girders in skyscrapers— in his head!—regularly bombed out on things like hair ribbons.

The party had started by the time Melba arrived. She'd been inwardly skipping to think of all the fun she'd have. She loved playing games and winning prizes. She adored ice cream and cake.

Already the front lawn was full of boys who were screaming and tackling each other on the grass. The girls were clumped together on the porch, laughing.

"Hey, look who's comin'!" shouted Tommy Lane, her number-one rival at Morton Elementary.

"Hi, Tommy," Melba called back with a smile. She held up Samuel's present. "Hope you didn't buy the same thing I did."

"No way, are you kidding? Hey, you guys, get a load of Melba! Some dress! You going to a coronation or what?"

"Look," Josh jumped in, "there's a Monarch butterfly on her hair. Somebody get a net!"

Melba reached up, for a second thinking she did have a butterfly on her head until her hand touched the stiff hairbow.

"Shut up, you creeps!" scolded Kim. "Come on, Melba. You look . . . far out. Really! Where'd you get the cute dress?"

"Young Fashions," she mumbled.

One glance was all it took to see she was farthest out of anybody. The other girls were in bicycle shorts and summer tops.

Melba took her gift into the house and said hello to Samuel's mother.

Outside, Tommy already had the boys screaming,

"Capture the Monster Monarch! Don't let it get away!" Her cheeks were burning. As soon as no one was looking, she tore the bow out of her hair and stuffed it into the wastebasket under the sink. One thing was sure: bigmouth Tommy hadn't grown any nicer over the summer.

Once they started playing Junior Trivia, however, Melba forgot to be embarrassed. She knew every answer.

"She has ESP," Tommy sneered. "She knows the answers before she even gets the questions."

"She's a witch!" Martin accused.

Kim gave Martin a shove that knocked him back on his heels. "You just can't stand to see the girls win, can you? Keep going, Melba!"

Her next card asked what the letters of the word *laser* stood for.

"Losers Are Sorrier Each Round," Tommy bellowed. The guys fell over laughing.

"Come on, Melba," Mary Belle coaxed, "you must know. Think."

Melba knew, all right, but she hesitated. It was no fun having the boys hate her because she was smart. She could throw the game their way if she wanted to, if she just pretended not to know.

About then, Tommy jumped up and pointed a finger at her head. "Psssssst! I'm frying your brains with a laser. Get the ketchup, Sammy, we're having fried brains. Oh, boy, yum-yum!"

That did it! With all the girls saying "Disgusting" and "He makes me sick," Melba knew she wasn't about to play dumb.

"The word *laser*," she said, staring a hole right through her tormentor, stands for 'light amplification by stimulated emission of radiation.' And," she added, chin up, "I also understand the principle."

Hands down, the girls won the Mars bars. Not only that, they sat and ate them in front of the boys, chomping and smacking their lips over every bite. Melba loved it.

"You're the star," Kim leaned over and whispered. "I'm glad we're friends."

Things didn't turn out so well on the geography game. Melba won all three prizes—including the red striped pencil case. And although she offered to share, the others acted as if they might be getting sick of her and her brains. Mrs. Dexter didn't smile handing her the last prize. "Enough's enough," her expression said.

"One more game," announced Samuel, tossing a basketball overhead, then failing to catch it. "The best shot gets a prize."

"All right!" Tommy yelled as he climbed over everyone to be the first outside. Everyone knew his dad was junior high coach. Since fourth grade he'd been Morton's best ball handler.

Melba missed her first two baskets. But so did Tommy—to everyone's surprise. And was he a sore loser. Pretty soon he was yelling "Cheat, cheat!" at whoever scored.

When it was Tommy's turn again, Melba screwed her face into her meanest expression, hoping he'd miss. He did! The ball thunked off the rim, then plunged into the shrubbery alongside the drive.

When Samuel's turn came, she wished the opposite. Samuel, like her, was terrible at ball games, but today he was hot. She watched as he dribbled raggedly toward the basket. He stopped, shoved up his glasses, took aim, shot.

"Miss, miss, miss!" the boys yelled to distract him.

Concentrating all her energies on the ball, Melba watched it rise in a beautiful arc, then fall with a nice swishing sound through the hoop.

Three baskets for Samuel! His guests were so stunned they broke into cheers. All except Tommy, who whipped out his gun finger and laser-melted Samuel Dexter on his own driveway.

Suddenly Melba realized what was happening. Without thinking, she was controlling the balls, the way she had during P.E. one time. It was her same old brain power! She alone had caused the girls' team to win the softball game that afternoon. Now she was making Samuel score and Tommy miss *without realizing she was doing it*. How scary! That kind of wish power was *dangerous*. Melba shivered in the hot sunlight. She positively must not throw her brain weight around like that.

In spite of her resolve, Melba's very next shot rolled twice around the rim, held for a second, then, to everyone's amazement, dropped through the net.

"Game's over!" Samuel's mother called from the kitchen window where she'd been watching. "Samuel's the winner. Inside for the movie, everyone."

Tommy grabbed up the ball and slammed it onto the driveway. "Way to go, Dexter! Don't you know it's stupid to give yourself a prize?"

Kim and Melba linked arms as they followed everyone into the house. "Is that Tommy Lane rude enough?" asked Kim under her breath.

Sammy didn't seem to care what any of his guests thought. He just grinned and tore the wrapping off the package. "I wanted these swim fins all along," he admitted as everyone laughed.

The video movie was funnier than anything, but all Melba could think about was what she had caused to happen. Was it brain power or wish power that had gotten out of hand? She couldn't always tell the difference. Or were Samuel's baskets a coincidence? Maybe he'd been practicing and Tommy hadn't. How would she know?

Her friends neither noticed nor cared when she scooted to a dark corner to bite her nails. What kind of school year would it be with brain power out of control . . . or wish power unlimited?

THE MUMMY

3

The Mummy Mix-up

The first Friday in October Melba's social studies classroom was a zoo. The new teacher—"Jake," as he liked to be called—had just walked into the room with a box labeled PLASTER-GAUZE FOR CASTS.

"Hear, hear, you dwellers by the Nile!" he greeted his students, a big smile showing through his beard. He motioned them to come in close. In seconds, everyone had crowded around the box to see what was inside.

For a whole week now Room 12 at Morton Elementary had been the Nile River Plain of ancient Egypt in the year 2144 B.C. Desks were pushed to each side to make room for the river, which, supposedly, ran down the middle. Half the students were living as farmers on the east bank of the Nile, and

14

half were stonecutters, carpenters, and slaves on the west. If they weren't raising wheat or goats on one side, they were building tombs and pyramids on the other.

But today the desks were against the wall and two oblong library tables occupied the middle of the room. Melba, like everyone else, was jumpy as jelly beans with excitement.

After taking roll, Jake held two essays up over his head and waited for all the *shushing* to stop. The authors of the two best essays would get to be "mummified," so to speak. Naturally, all the kids were dying to be mummies. All but Mary Belle, that is.

"You couldn't pay me," she said, terrified of the whole idea. "I'd stop breathing in there, I know I would."

Carefully, using only his fingertips, the teacher rolled out the first winning scroll. "Very old papyrus," he joked when the paper crackled.

"The girls' essay chosen by the judges is number— um—looks like eleven. On your feet, young lady. Let's see who you are."

Melba stood, her cheeks on fire, thrilled to the soles of her sneakers.

"Yea, Melba!" cheered Mary Belle. The other girls in the class groaned with disappointment

"Excellent essay," Jake complimented her. "You get to be the pharaoh's favorite wife."

"Who's the lucky pharaoh?" asked a smart aleck.

"I'm about to tell you. The winning essay for the boys is . . ." He rolled the scroll out slowly to prolong the suspense. "Number two."

Tommy's gagging sounds let everyone know who had won.

"I resign," he yelled, making like he was sick. "Someone else can be pharaoh."

"Nope!" Jake raised a hand for order. "Once a pharaoh, always a pharaoh. All right, you two, hop up on those tables. We've got a big job ahead of us. In ancient Egypt, preparing a body took two months. We have"—he glanced at his watch—"a little less than two hours before school's out."

Quickly, the teacher chose a committee and sent two students to bring buckets of water. The others got busy cutting the stiff strips of plaster-gauze into lengths. The "stonecutters" went back to work on their Styrofoam pyramid and the "artists" returned to painting gold jewelry. Next week the glittering necklaces and earrings would be placed in the royal sepulchers.

Lying flat on their backs on the two tables, Melba and Tommy exchanged nervous looks. "Watch out for the deadly asp!" she whispered.

Tommy let out a cry, pulled an imaginary asp off his neck, stiffened, and died.

She giggled—until he threw the snake on her!

The first thing Jake did was spread a plastic sheet over their shirts, jeans, and shoes, leaving heads and hands exposed. Looking down the length of her body, Melba was glad she wouldn't be wrapped all the way around like a real mummy. The plan today was to make two mummy cases that would be lifted off their bodies once they hardened. She and Tommy were simply the models. Monday they'd paint on hands, faces, and hair, and would decorate the cases for the funeral trip down the Nile.

Melba shivered with excitement. Social studies had never been so much fun.

In a minute Jake was smearing Vaseline on Tommy's hands and between his fingers, making him laugh. Melba, too, squealed when he slathered the cold, slimy protection on her skin.

He then placed her hands, one across the other, over her chest. "You have to lie very still now. If your nose itches, ask someone to scratch it, you hear?"

Suddenly Melba itched all over. And her leg wanted to jiggle. She looked across to see Tommy's chest heaving as he grabbed big breaths through his mouth. He was nervous, too.

As luck would have it, Mary Belle was the one assigned to cover Melba's hair with a cotton wig—so the head shape of the case would come out right. Pulling and tugging the huge wad of cotton into

place, Mary Belle never stopped talking about suffo-
cating. If Melba's hands hadn't been slick with Vaseline, she'd have punched her.

The plastering itself began at their shoes. Melba's
group dunked the plaster-gauze in the buckets, then,
a strip at a time, carefully laid and overlapped the
cloths.

A few minutes into the process, Melba looked
down to find that her feet had disappeared. Another
half hour and her legs were covered. Now she really
did get the heebie-jeebs, imagining all sorts of crawly
things on her skin.

The kids on the committee were having a big old
time because *they* weren't inside all the plastic and
gunk. They'd tickle the mummy models to make
them laugh, then yell if they moved so much as a
millimeter.

"How we gonna breathe when you cover our
faces?" Melba asked.

"Mummies don't breathe," Jake answered, winking
at Tommy.

"Yeah, stupid," came the pharaoh's voice. "You
won't be breathing at all once they push that hook
up your nose and take out your brains. Hah, hah! I
love it. Melba the Brainless."

The others thought that was verrrry funny, but
Melba just stuck out her tongue. She wondered if
writing the winning essay was worth it. Who'd want

to share an afterlife with Tommy Lane, anyway? Seeing him at school was bad enough.

"Hey!" she called finally to anyone listening. "I'm burning up in here!"

"Gag her," whooped Tommy from his table. "The queen talks too much."

The pharaoh had his way. Along came their teacher with his oversized Vaseline jar. Another treatment. This time her eyes and mouth were sealed shut and jell was smeared over her entire face. Then someone pushed a straw between her lips.

"Breathe through your mouth and nose both so you'll get enough air," Jake told her.

Melba decided her team was farther along than Tommy's. She couldn't say a word once her mouth was stuck shut, but he continued to yak away.

"What will you do without your famous brains?" he taunted her.

"Mmmmmmmm, umm, mmmmm!"

"You'll need a new name. How about Melba the Pain? Yeah, I like that. It's painful just looking at you!"

Even inside the goopy Vaseline, Melba's eyes started to sting. He could hurt her feelings more in one minute than anyone else could in a year.

"Leave her nostrils clear," came Jake's voice as someone pinched a gauze strip around her nose. Eye sockets next, the plaster feeling cold and oozy on her skin. *Take it easy!* she wanted to scream when someone pushed too hard on her eyeballs.

More strips, layer after layer. Finally, just when Melba decided she couldn't stand mummification one more minute, Jake was back speaking at her ear. "Now comes the hard part," he told her. "We have to let the plaster set. So relax and concentrate on something nice. You're doing great, kiddo!"

Melba sucked in air, pushed it out again. Inhale, exhale. *Relax. Don't panic.*

Astrocat! She'd think of Astrocat. She had worried about him all summer as it was. Months had passed since he'd been to Earth. She thought of his indiscreet babbling and the way his dear whiskers quivered when she'd first accused him of being a spy. Was he still the proprietor of Jelly Bean Junction, the sweet-smelling candy factory?

She thought of Boss Cat, too, the queen disguised as king on the planet where animals rule Uprights. Gruffy old Boss Cat, who knew more CB talk than her father's trucker friends. She could see them all—Gotcha Gator, the eagles who thought they were her foster parents, the bionic frog. Even the funny little ants, who had made her feel better when she was lost.

"They're covering my mouth, Melba!" Tommy broke the quiet. "My last words are 'I hate you!' "

There was no stinging of tears for Melba this time.

Bug off! she thought fiercely. *They'd teach you the Golden Rule in a hurry on the Animals' Planet! You should be an endangered species!*

What seemed a couple of dynasties later, Melba's team began freeing the mummy case from her body. She could feel the cold metal spatula underneath her arms, then a rush of air as the plastic was loosened all around. The case made cracking, squeaking noises as it was lifted off, and then she could see light beneath her eyelids again.

Melba blinked through Vaseline lashes at the ring of faces bent over her. She gulped in the cool air and smiled.

"Hooray, the mummy lives!" cried Samuel Dexter as the other kids whooped and slapped each other's hands and danced around. The stonemasons and artists left their work and came over, everyone excited.

Karen shoved Kleenex in her hand as soon as she sat up. Somebody else pulled off pieces of cotton wig and straightened her T-shirt. With hands patting her from every direction, Melba thought, it was like having a whole bunch of mothers fussing over her. She loved it.

At that moment the bell rang, sending Jake rushing around the room.

"Bus students, take off," he shouted. "If some of you can give me a hand cleaning up, I'll appreciate it."

Melba's team grabbed the tissue box and trotted off to the girls' room. Now that it was over, she could laugh and say things like "No, it was neat in there" and "Can you believe I had a heartbeat in my ears?"

On the way back, Melba heard a lot of excited talk coming from Room 12.

Mary Belle was shouting, "Jake, come here! He isn't breathing!"

"He is, too," Martin insisted, his eye at the straw as he tried to peek in. "Make a noise in there, Tommy. She thinks you're dead."

By then half a dozen kids were surrounding the table. Melba reached out and held her hand above the straw. Nothing. But then, he could be breathing through his nose. Knowing Tommy . . . of course!

"Stop holding your breath," she ordered near his ear.

Jake didn't act worried. He knocked on the case, saying, "Grunt if you're okay."

There was no sound from inside, not even a grunt. The kids' eyes widened when their teacher bent down to inspect the case, then said, "Who's been messing with this?" The whole thing had slid along the table, leaving two inches of white track behind.

"Quick!" Jake sprang into action. "Get him out."

Melba stood back, hands over her mouth, her legs suddenly weak.

In seconds, the teacher and Martin loosened and lifted the mummy case, bringing the plastic up with it.

Melba gasped. Tommy wasn't there! The mummy case was empty.

"Oh, no!" came a cry from Mary Belle, whose face had gone white as plaster.

Jake's shoulders sagged with relief. "That little scamp!" he said with a laugh. "He let himself out. Now, why would he do that? Check the boys' room, you guys, and see if you can find him. We're lucky he didn't ruin things."

"He rides the bus," Samuel called back as he trotted off to look for Tommy. "Bet he didn't want to walk home in the rain."

Inside the wrappings, Melba hadn't noticed the rain that was now blowing in sheets against the windows.

She didn't want to get wet, either, but she knew by the goose bumps rising on her arms that Tommy wasn't on the bus *or* in the building. What horrible thing had she done to him? Staring at his dead-white likeness on the table, Melba suddenly felt sick to her stomach.

"I'll go call Mom," Kim told Melba and the other girls who had stayed to clean up. "She'll come and get us."

Later, as the carful of girls chattered away about

the fun they'd had, Melba pushed herself deeper into the cushions of the backseat and worried.

The boys hadn't found Tommy, but that didn't surprise her. She knew he hadn't let himself out of that mummy case. She knew it as surely as she knew she was on planet Earth . . . in her best friend's car . . . on the first Friday of October.

By now, Tommy was on Outpost Ouch—she was sure of it!—at the mercy of animals who enjoyed keeping Uprights in their place.

4

Panic in the Pyramid

"Thanks for the ride," Melba shouted as she got out
of Kim's car. "See you Monday." She dashed up the
driveway through the rain.

Inside, she headed straight for the kitchen phone.
She punched out Tommy's number, then stood there
shaking water out of her hair through four long rings.

"Mrs. Lane?" she asked breathlessly. "This is
Melba. Is Tommy home?"

"Not yet," came his mother's voice, "but I wasn't
expecting him this soon. He's with a friend. He'll be
here for dinner, of course."

Of course. Oh, brother!

"But could you tell me whose house? I need to ask
him a question about social studies."

Mrs. Lane went on and on about what a switch

25

that was—Melba asking Tommy to explain anything. Finally she said he was playing video games with Martin.

Melba was pretty sure he wasn't. Martin was at school when she left, helping the teacher. She tried Martin's number anyway.

No answer.

Discouraged, Melba leaned against the wall. She stared at Boots, who had stationed himself in front of her, his tail swinging like a jump rope.

Dinnertime! his eyes reminded her.

Ignoring Boots's hopeful expression, Melba pounced on the phone again.

"Is this Anthony?" she asked a second later. "You usually take the school bus, don't you? I'm trying to find Tommy. Was he on the bus this afternoon?"

Anthony thought a minute, then said, "Nope, I don't think so. How come you want him? I thought you and Tommy hated each other."

"Oh, we do, but I need to ask him something. Well, thanks."

The prickles on Melba's scalp grew as big as artichokes. What had she done? Poor Tommy!

But maybe Anthony was mistaken. She tried other phone numbers, speaking to Jason, Imogene, and Mark, all bus riders. No one remembered seeing Tommy after school.

Without giving her dog a single pat, Melba

spooned food into one side of his dish and splashed water into the other. "There now, eat!" she said, sounding snappish even to herself. She tossed the spoon into the sink and whirled out of the room.

Two seconds later, she was in the den seated in front of the computer.

Click, hummmmm. She got things going.

She fingered through the disk organizer for one marked OUTPOST OUCH, then slipped it into drive B and waited for the whirring to stop. Thank heavens she'd programmed her breakthrough formulas into their new Technolite XL-600! At the time, she'd promised herself never to use her startling knowledge again unless there was an emergency.

So now you've got one! screamed her brain.

Entering OO, the code name for Outpost Ouch, Melba brought the right file to the screen. She paged down . . . down . . . down . . . checking figures.

Suddenly the yellow numbers in front of her began to slide off the screen, the way things dissolved and disappeared on *Sesame Street.* Melba shrank away. What was happening?

Over the humming of the machine came a piercingly sharp *bleep, bleep, bleep!* She covered her ears. Not a virus! There were hundreds of viruses infecting people's computers. "Oh, please, not now!"

A shimmering figure burned into her screen from somewhere. Astrocat! In his same old space suit and helmet. Hairs stood on Melba's arms. What was going on?

Wobbly letters appeared next. They joined to become words, spilling out of the cat's mouth and dropping to the bottom of the screen, where they bounced, then righted themselves to become a message.

TOMMY LANE CLAIMS TO BE PHARAOH, Melba read, her eyes round as dinner plates. BOSS CAT FURIOUS! EMBALMING TOMORROW UNLESS . . .

"Unless what?" Melba shrieked when the words quit coming. "Go on, don't stop!"

The image began to fade. She pounded the space bar. The bleeps grew more and more faint until they, too, were gone. And then, *whap*! The computer went dead. Her dear friend, Astrocat, had given her only part of a message.

Melba slumped over the keyboard. Just as she feared, she'd sent bigmouth Tommy to the Animals' Planet. He wouldn't be safe there. He had no respect. And Gotcha Gator's powerful jaws were fresh as yesterday in her memory. How could a great break-through person like herself have been so careless with her powers?

Melba's heart was really drumming in her ears now.

If she hadn't lost everything in the computer

blackout, the original coordinates—safe in the memory—would work the necessary magic. All she had to do, once she was ready, was push the key marked "Escape." The microchips and her own brain power would do the rest—the amazing rest, which would put her on Outpost Ouch.

Melba shuddered to remember that Uprights like Tommy and herself were merely servants and pets on the Animals' Planet. Sometimes—as Astrocat had hinted darkly—even *worse*.

Luck was with her. Working fast, Melba called up the egress formula. She pressed "Escape," then tore through the house to get to her back porch. Standing there, wishing with all her might to be on Astrocat's planet, she emitted such powerful brain waves that her arms and legs began to tremble.

Thunder crashed. A searing light bleached the landscape of her yard.

The formulas are working!

In one fractured second she was sucked—not into a black hole as before—but into what she instantly knew was one of the astronomers' newly discovered "worm holes." The minutest of tubes, a hole in the fabric of time and space, was siphoning her away into the universe.

What a sensation, the elongating of her atoms as she spun farther and farther from Earth, stretched to the merest thread! Only Boots's long, mournful howl followed her into the tunnel of the unknown.

Later—or earlier, time being what it is in space— Melba came to rest.

Where was she? She hadn't the slightest idea, or even *if* she still existed. Testing, she lifted a finger, then a hand. So far, so good. She was lying on her back on a hard surface—a hard, cold surface. She shivered and tried hugging herself, which wasn't easy, jammed in as she was.

Melba sniffed at the air around her. The smells were musty, reminding her of her grandmother's basement. At least she could breathe.

Pushing up her glasses, she peered into the shadowy dark. It felt as if she were in some kind of container. The insides were rough, like stone, and the sides were thick. Her stomach did a number on the rest of her when she realized the container was exactly her size.

Quickly she sat up, glad there wasn't a lid. As her eyes adjusted, she could see she was sitting alone in the center of a small room. The ceiling was peaked, the stony walls around her were gray and bare.

"Where am I?" she asked aloud, terrified, but needing to hear her own voice. "Huh?" she tried again.

"Huh, huh, huh?" came the echoes.

"Anybody home?" She hoped Gotcha Gator wasn't crawling around somewhere. Not in this scary place without the protection of a cage or anything.

There was no answer.

Braver now, Melba climbed out of whatever-it-was. On closer inspection it did look like a stone coffin, and it was her size. Was it meant for her?

Melba crept toward the faint light that washed in from a doorway. She peered into the adjoining room. It was even smaller, but at least it was furnished.

"Baseball stuff!" she exclaimed, recognizing balls, bats, and a mitt in the dim light of the oil lamp.

She picked a stack of cards off a shelf, flipped through them to find pictures of Babe Ruth, Mickey Mantle, other baseball greats. On another shelf were games—Junior Pictionary and Monopoly, of all things. Was she in someone's trendy game room?

Turning around, Melba nearly leaped out of her bones. There on the wall was an enormous photograph of Jake, the new teacher at Morton Elementary, smiling big as life. "Whaaaat?" she said aloud. "What *is* this?"

She stepped close to read what was on the brass plate under the picture. FAVORITE TEACHER it said in ordinary English.

She spotted a brightly painted jar next that was nearly as tall as she was. It would do for hiding, if it came to that. Melba stood on her tiptoes to see if it was empty.

"Jelly beans!" she exclaimed. "In rainbow colors." She thrust in a hand and gave them a good stirring. "My favorite candy."

What did it mean, the picture, the games, the candy? At least she wouldn't starve while she was here.

A low, square tunnel led out from the second room, but the dark was so fierce Melba could see only a few feet into the passageway. Suddenly she swung around. She eyed the walls of massive stone blocks that fit perfectly along hairline cracks . . . the two rooms, one smaller, the other larger . . . the favorite things . . .

Serious goose bumps rose on her skin as the diagram from her social studies textbook flashed to mind. Figure 22, page 133 of the chapter on ancient Egypt.

"I knew it!" Melba exclaimed as everything came together. "That—that stone coffin! It's my sarcophagus."

Whirling around to face the games, she cried, "And these are the things I loved during my . . . life! I've been entombed. Like a mummy, only I'm still alive. These are burial rooms beneath a pyramid. What happened? I meant to send myself to the Animals' Planet, but I never left Earth at all!"

"Is anyone here?" she cried out. "Help! I'm not a real mummy. No way! Are you here, Tommy?"

"Tommeeeeeeee," echoed the chilly chamber, making her feel more alone than ever.

5

Alone in the Tunnel

Ominous! Melba bit her lip, remembering the new word from Thursday's vocabulary study. Having a sneak preview of her own burial was nothing short of ominous.

She rubbed her cold arms and peered into the blackness of the tunnel. If she really was beneath a pyramid, that tunnel should be the passage to the outside. *If* it hadn't been sealed off. The idea put prickles on her scalp. Being a dummy mummy had been bad enough; she didn't want to be a real one.

For a while she just stood there, listening for sounds. Finally she lifted the oil lamp out of its stand. "Exploring's better than waiting around for the embalming crew," she said in a shaky voice, then ducked and entered the tunnel.

Darkness closed behind her like so many doors, sealing off the two burial chambers. Feeling her way with one hand, she crept forward, now and then flinching when her hair brushed the ceiling. For once, she was glad to be kid size. An ordinary adult would be bent double.

Soon she was able to stand straight and walk a little faster.

On and on she went, finding every inch the same. She'd stop to listen, to catch her breath. She'd swing around and peer into the dark, as if someone or some*thing* might be following her.

"How long does this go on?" she asked, to hear her own voice. A perfectly straight tunnel had to go somewhere, didn't it?

Suddenly the passage began to incline. Walking grew harder, as if she were climbing stairs . . . and breathing was harder.

She had just started thinking about taking a rest when she noticed the flame bobbing from side to side. She cupped her hand around it. There must be a draft coming in from somewhere.

Melba set down the lamp and took a few cautious steps ahead into the dark. Yes, there! A light—dim as early dawn—still yards ahead. Was it coming from outside? She hurried on, excited by the smells of fresh air. It must be daylight she was seeing!

Melba began to run, sure finally that the long,

frightening tunnel was coming to an end. She was right. There, looming in front of her, framed by a square opening, was a rosy-pink sky.

She rushed out of the tunnel and into the open. "This can't be Egypt!" she shouted, blinking into the strong light. The sky was the same peachy-pink color she remembered from her other visits to the planet. And below, on both sides of the river, were *blue* leaves on the palm trees, the fronds lifting in the breeze like so many weird hairpieces.

"It's Outpost Ouch, it has to be. I *am* back on the Animals' Planet."

Across the river she could see tents and mud-colored dwellings. A village, she guessed. Beyond that, sand dunes stretched forever. She had to shade her eyes, the light was so brilliant.

Turning and looking up, she gasped to see the massive pyramid that was towering over her. It took a dozen steps backward to get a decent look.

"Hey, the top's missing," she exclaimed, laughing in spite of her fears. "It's not finished yet."

In the distance stood three more pyramids, looking exactly like the ones pictured in her social studies textbook. If she were color-blind—if she couldn't tell green from blue or pink—she'd swear her new Technolite computer had dropped her on the Nile River Plain.

Melba grinned. Nothing on this crazy planet should surprise her. Not really. Boss Cat and her subjects were experts at copying whatever suited them from Earth. She remembered the back porch they'd built, a duplicate from her own at home, but so far as she knew, no one had ever bothered to add a house.

Just then Melba noticed a signpost off to her right that seemed to be some sort of directory. The topmost board pointing to the farthest pyramid said KING SNAFU. Queen Tofu resided in the small pyramid nearby, according to the next sign on the post. Melba wrinkled her nose. Here, as in the time of pharaohs, she guessed, queens had to settle for less.

The last pyramid on the horizon belonged to Sop-It-Up the Great. Melba laughed outright. Who could get serious about a king whose name was Sop-It-Up?

In her two trips to the planet, Melba had visited lots of different places, but she'd never been here. Arriving in the desert among pyramids was like stumbling onto a Hollywood movie set, for crying out loud!

Quickly, she took in the scene below. A barge was moving downriver, a long boat with oarsmen. Or oarswomen. Here on the Animals' Planet, most likely oars*beasts*, but she couldn't be sure. Across the river, in and around the tents, were paths and trees and what looked like a public well in the center of things. She wondered what little animals were scurrying in and out of the shops, putting up awnings. Melba frowned. She had to remind herself that she was no tourist. She had come to find Tommy and take him back to Earth. No matter that he made her life miserable at Morton Elementary. It was her fault that he was in trouble eighty light-years from home.

With her legs fighting slow motion, a condition Uprights experience on the Animals' Planet, Melba headed downhill toward the river.

"Tommy Lane claims to be pharaoh." She went over Astrocat's message again and again, forcing her brain to make connections. "Boss Cat furious. Embalming tomorrow unless . . ."

Knowing that Astrocat was her only real friend on the planet, she'd look for him first. No doubt he'd put himself in danger to smuggle a warning to her.

"Oh, my gosh!" Melba gasped as an idea brought her to a stop. Could the burial preparations be for Tommy, not her? The baseball things, the favorite teacher, the sarcophagus *her* size. Tommy's size, too. She'd been so scared, she'd simply assumed she was the one to be mummified.

But what about the jelly beans? came a voice from within.

Melba shrugged and ran on. All kids loved jelly beans, didn't they?

She only hoped she was in time. Her Majesty, with or without a mane, was no pussycat. Tommy's life wasn't worth a royal pomegranate if he crossed the mighty Boss Cat.

MELBA THE MUMMY

6

Boss Cat's Barter

Melba tore downhill to the river, still without a clue as to how she'd get across. There wasn't a bridge anywhere, and she'd suddenly begun to hear clattering noises on the path behind her.

She took a frantic dive into a thicket of rushes that grew alongside the river. Instantly she sank up to her ankles in mud. Another worry! What if she lost her shoes?

Crouching out of sight, Melba peered through the tall reeds. Just in time. A family of goats—*goats*, of all things!—came trotting past, heading for the river.

Like parents, the two bigger ones seemed to be in charge. The rest, she guessed, were their kids. Anyway, the younger ones acted like kids—shoving, biting, kicking up their heels. The tiniest goat, busy singing a little tune, arrived last. *What a cute pet, that one!* thought Melba, forgetting for a minute that animals on this planet weren't anybody's pets.

She straightened to get a better view.

Bleating instructions, the older, bearded one brought the others close. She heard him say, "It's your turn, Baby Goat. Go let the crocodile birds know we're ready."

Melba looked on in amazement. She'd never get used to hearing animals talk, not in a dozen dynasties. She couldn't believe she was hiding in the bulrushes eavesdropping on goats, hoping to find a way across the river.

All at once, the words *crocodile birds* soaked in. If there were crocodile birds, there'd also be . . . *ulp!* Quickly, she searched the swampy grass around her ankles.

She looked back in time to see Baby Goat skip happily across the clearing to the water's edge. Lifting her pink nose, she bleated out a message, then waited, tail switching, as a cloud of birds rose from the riverbanks and circled overhead.

A glance toward the river, and Melba sucked in her breath. A string of crocodiles—big ones!—were rising to the surface of the water. Their bodies, tail to snout, formed a line all the way to the other side.

The goats were now prancing about, butting for position. Younger ones first, they went leaping over

the backs of the reptiles as if they were stepping
stones. It was a sight for the record books: a bridge
of leathery, mud-colored crocodiles.

Melba's heart began to pound. There wasn't time
to be scared. She pulled her sneakers free and fought
her way out of the bulrushes. Memories of Gotcha
Gator and his terrible teeth swiped at her, but she
had to take chances if she was to find Tommy. Lucky
for her, the eyes of the overgrown lizards faced the
other way. Maybe they'd think she was one of the
goats.

Melba followed the biggest and heaviest of the lot
onto the strange bridge, panicked at first by her mud-
slick shoes. Thinking surefooted, goat-footed thoughts,
she high-stepped from one crocodile to another,
springing over the last two or three as the bridge
disappeared behind her.

"Made it!" she exclaimed breathlessly at the opposite bank. The crocodiles and their sleepy eyes van-
ished into the water as noiselessly as they'd appeared.

Already the family of goats was trotting off, all
except the young one who remained behind to stare.

"That's just a robot," a sibling called over its tail.
"Come on."

By then Baby Goat was nuzzling Melba's hand, as
if looking for a treat. "You used to be my baby-
sitter," she said in a shy voice.

"Your what?" Melba asked, astonished.

"My baby-sitter. When I was little. You brought jelly beans, don't you remember?" Giggling like any kid, Baby Goat scooted off along the trail the others had taken.

Melba stood there flabbergasted . . . until she *did* remember.

"Of course!" she said under her breath. "They think I'm Melba-the-Robot. They think I belong here."

She'd been so worried about herself and Tommy, she'd forgotten she had an exact double on this planet: a robot who looked like her, who talked like her, who was her mirror image. A clone, so to speak, who'd been programmed for serving the animals. Already she felt better.

She remembered what fun Melba-the-Robot had had the one day Boss Cat allowed her a trip to Earth. She, the original Melba, had let her win the spelling bee at school, had let her do all the crazy things she'd always wished she could do. Now, thinking about it, she hoped she'd been nice enough to Melba-the-Robot.

Melba took off running, kicking up sand with every step. She had a hunch the goats would lead her to the village she'd spotted, where she hoped to find Tommy. If only she wasn't too late!

On the way she ran past low-slung mud-colored dwellings that didn't look like anything humans could live in. Down one twisty lane, she disturbed a neighborhood of chickens that screeched and flew in her face, scaring her half to death.

She was glad finally to come into what seemed to be the town square or marketplace. She had to enter under a flapping twenty-foot banner that swung between two palm trees. BOSS CAT'S BARTER, it said in plain English.

ARTS, CRAFTS, MISFORTUNES, RECYCLED REAL ESTATE,
CAMEL RACE, HIPPO HUNT
BRING YOUR OLD STUFF, GET SOME NEW STUFF
STUFF ENOUGH FOR ALL!

Melba smiled in spite of herself. So Boss Cat was still in charge, and the barter was an old-fashioned country fair. Or a swap meet.

With cautious steps, she entered the square itself, which was mobbed with animals—a few she didn't recognize, some speaking languages she didn't understand. Acrid smells reached her nostrils and the smoke of cook fires made her eyes water. Her hope was to blend into the jostling, braying crowd until she could find Astrocat, but everything was so strange she almost lost her nerve.

"Don't touch the robot!" a cow said, warning her calf aside. "You'll catch something."

Good! thought Melba, hoping they'd all feel the

same. It was a weird experience, being mistaken for her look-alike. And terrifying, to think she was alone in such a confusing place. Knowing that Uprights on Earth had caused the extinction of entire animal species, she dared not hope for a welcome here.

The first booth Melba saw was one overflowing with animal antlers. Hundreds of them, all shapes and sizes. It wasn't the antlers that gave her the shivers, however; it was the sleek rodents crawling in and out of the pile, over and under and around everything.

"Step right up for a good gnaw!" barked a portly rat who was leaning against a ball of string three times his size. When a rat or mouse decided on a particular antler, the merchant rat would get his teeth going and chew off a length of string. He was so busy tending his merchandise, he never once looked her way.

Melba watched in fascination as the rodents tied up their antlers and dragged them off. They looked like so many little oxen hitched to plows.

"Home to the sewerburbs," one of them said to her as he huffed by.

"Mine's bigger than yours!" squeaked a tiny one that looked like a hamster.

Melba hurried on. Talking animals were so interesting. She'd have to be careful. After all, she was an Upright. It was true that Boss Cat had once dubbed her Honorary Beast, but that was at the birthday banquet where everyone was being nice. Sooner or later she'd be discovered for who she was. It just mustn't happen before she found Tommy.

Melba took refuge at the edge of a cooking tent, her eyes ranging over the crowd. He'd stand out, Tommy would: he was taller than the heads of most animals. Her heart sank when she didn't see another Upright anywhere.

Just then Melba felt herself being jostled. "Hey, whoa!" she cried as three heavy oxen crashed out of the brush behind her. She jumped aside, but a horn grazed her elbow, leaving her more scared than ever.

She'd better look for Astrocat first, she decided, tearfully rubbing the red place on her arm. She mustn't lose her cool. Not now. If he hadn't been decked by Boss Cat, he'd likely have a jelly bean concession right here somewhere. All she had to do was find him. He'd lead her to Tommy, she knew.

Shaky though she was, Melba made herself go back to the activity in the square. Maybe she could ask a question or two. For sure, no one seemed to be afraid of her.

COOKOO'S RECYCLING CENTER was the next booth she came to. The hashed-out sign looked as if it might have been recycled once too often.

Peeking in, Melba saw dozens of birds' nests hanging from a makeshift ceiling. Most were ordinary stickery nests such as she'd seen on Earth, but a few were apartment-style units, honeycombed with holes. Nests as big as tractor tires were stacked at one side. Melba reached out to touch one, then quickly drew back her hand. She'd never forget how the eagles pushed her out of their nest.

The birds in charge—world-class yakkers—didn't give her a chance to ask about Astrocat. Just as well. Birds and cats mightn't like each other here any more than they did on Earth.

Hurrying on, Melba was nonetheless impressed by the animals' recycling. Why waste a perfectly good nest? Or an antler, for that matter. Her dad and she felt the same. They were recycling all kinds of things at home.

Real estate booth signs featured WATERFRONT PROPERTY, BURROWS FOR RENT, QUIET NEIGHBORHOODS. She went by them without stopping, her eyes still ranging over the crowd. She definitely wasn't interested in acquiring property on Outpost Ouch.

Past a watering trough and on through a herd of sheep, Melba made her way to the other side of the busy square. There, swinging in front of an adobe building, was a gilt-framed sign written in English and hieroglyphics both.

DR. GOTCHUR-GRIN GATOR
PAINLESS ADJUSTMENTS AND EXTRACTIONS

So Gotcha Gator was still an orthodontist. Instead of gnashing teeth in the Royal Gator Guard, he was now busy straightening them. *How nice*, Melba thought with pride. Her father's calculator, left behind on the planet, had undoubtedly helped him learn his math.

Excited by so much that was new and different, Melba had to force herself again to remember why she was on the planet. When she did, it was as if an immense purple and white striped tent rose up right in front of her. It had been there all along, of course, but she hadn't really noticed it.

One beautiful word, *INFORMATION*, flew on a flag above the tent. Melba sighed with relief. Information was just what she needed most.

A note on the tent flap mentioned that the Society for the Preservation of Uprights was also housed inside. What luck! The S.P.U. must be an animal group that helped Uprights, the way the Humane Society on Earth helped animals. Finally she had a lead.

Melba lifted the tent flap and walked in. Her eyes hadn't quite adjusted to the dark when she felt herself lashed sharply around the middle and whisked off her feet.

"Yeeeeii!" she screamed as she went flying through the air.

"You sniveling snip of insubordination!" roared a deep voice. "I've been waiting for you."

Melba, having landed facedown in a pile of cushions, now opened her eyes to find herself nose to jowls with the biggest lion she'd ever seen.

Back into the pillows she went.

"Look at me, you miserable mite!"

Somehow, Melba managed to sit up. "I beg your pardon—" she whispered. What had she done that was so terrible?

By now the tawny lion had leaped back across the table, far enough away so Melba could see its outlandish attire. In place of a mane—or over it, she couldn't tell which—the lion wore a turban, a giant beehive of a turban that sparkled like stars at midnight. A cape hung carelessly off one shoulder. If it came to a contest, Melba was mincemeat.

"I beg your pardon, s-s-sir . . ." she muttered.

"Can't you get anything right?" the big cat roared. "Do I look like a *sir* in this getup?"

The lioness looked like a Gypsy fortune-teller, but Melba wasn't about to say that.

She tried again. "Really, I'm sorry."

"Sorrrrrrry!" The lion mocked her. "What kind of talk is that? In the history of robotics, there's never been a sorry robot. What I want to know is, who nibbled the corners off my tuna turnovers this morning?"

"Oh, not I, ma'am . . ."

"Then who is the brainy little beast, " she snarled, "who keeps beating me in Trivial Conceits? Tell me that. In two hundred and nineteen games, I haven't won once."

Trivial Conceits? Melba's head was spinning. She'd try another tack.

"Please," she ventured, "could I talk to someone in the Society for the Preservation of Uprights?"

"The P.U.? Never mind, they're working on your case right now."

"Really?" Melba said, making big eyes. "Oh, that's nice."

"Yes, indeedy. A few years down the galaxy—after the Uprights have destroyed Earth—we'll have a specimen of the human body for our scientists to study." She chuckled deep in her throat. "You've been marked for preservation by an ancient Upright method. And I won't miss you a millimeter. You never once made my catnip tea the way I like it."

Melba leaped to her feet. "You mean *that* kind of preservation? You mean the pyramid and the sepulcher are for me?"

The lioness snatched up her tail and went to work fanning her face.

"Who else? I'm having a sphinx built for myself.

But now that you're here, let's have a seance or something. I just love chronicling gloom and doom!" She tsk-tsk'd a few times. "The poor, stupid Uprights. They never learn, do they?"

Melba was really confused now. The burial preparations weren't for Tommy *or* her. The sepulcher and the favorite things were for Melba-the-Robot. That would explain the jelly beans, since she and her double had identical tastes. Unless she missed her guess, the robot was being punished for poor service as well as being preserved for scientific study.

From somewhere among the pillows the lioness snatched up a fortune-teller's glass ball and smacked it down on the table between them.

"Four-on-the-floor and a big ten-four!" she growled at the crystal ball, which instantly crackled to life.

Melba slumped into the cushions, weak as a reed. She no longer needed a program to know who was under that turban and cape. Once again she was face-to-face with Boss Cat, Queen of Beasts on Outpost Ouch. And *she* was being mistaken for a royal slave. She had played the part of Melba-the-Robot too well.

7

The Gloom Sayer

"I'm not a fortune-teller, if that's what you're thinking," said Boss Cat.

That's exactly what Melba was thinking. For the moment, however, she couldn't take her eyes off what was happening inside the crystal ball. A storm was brewing. Miniature thunderheads were piling up everywhere. Every few seconds, lightning bursts electrified Boss Cat's features, making her look scarier than ever.

"If you're not a fortune-teller, what are you?" ventured Melba.

"I'm a *mis*fortune teller, dummy! I concentrate on the present." A smug purr came from her throat. "That way I'm always right."

"Good thinking!" Melba said, impressed. "So . . .

with all due respect, could you tell me what's happening in that ball?"

"If you were an Upright instead of a robot, I'd tell you plenty."

"But I am an Upright," Melba said, forgetting. "I mean," she bit her lip, "I'm related to an Upright. Sort of."

"Our spies," Madam Misfortune confided, "do a very thorough job of monitoring the mess Uprights are making of their planet."

Melba jumped in. "Is Astrocat still in the spy business?"

"That dozing dud of a doodlebug? No way!"

The curtains behind Boss Cat shook violently, making Melba think for a minute that someone was back there. By then Boss Cat was stroking the ball with her huge paws and muttering things, so Melba had to watch. Melba-the-Robot might be marked for preservation, but there didn't seem to be any big hurry about it.

"Would you mind"—Melba said bravely—"telling me what you'd tell an Upright? I was on Earth once, you remember, at Morton Elementary."

"A big mistake that was!" Boss Cat muttered. "Spelling bees—ugh!" She gave the glass a good polishing with her cloak, complaining the whole time about how "dirty" Earth had become. "The Uprights go merrily along, choking themselves to death with

Ivy Ruckman

particulates. I sometimes have a job finding the place."

Melba nodded soberly. Her father talked the same way.

"Aha, a peephole!" Boss Cat pounced, pushing an eye right down against the surface of the ball. "A break in the ozone layer! I see you now, you Earthling idiots, thanks to your chlorofluorocarbons."

Melba felt weird listening to such talk. What a gloom sayer! Desperately she wanted to peek at Earth herself, but Boss Cat stayed hunkered over the crystal ball and wouldn't share.

"Oh, my aching astrologies!" Madam Misfortune gasped a bit later. "Another school of whales have beached themselves."

"Oh no!" cried Melba. "Why do they *do* that?"

"Don't you know?" the big cat looked up in surprise. "They're making a protest. The oceans—mercy! Chemicals, oil spills, the whole kit and caboodle out of balance. How else can they protest when they can't talk? They simply throw themselves on the beach to die."

Melba stared. Not once had she tried thinking about the whales' beaching as a protest, but it made sense now that Boss Cat pointed it out.

More interested than ever, Melba leaned forward just in time to see the crystal ball go all wet and steamy. Droplets formed, then went streaming down inside the globe.

"Oh, drat!" Boss Cat spat out the words. "That always happens."

"What always happens? What do you mean?"

"With Earth becoming a steaming greenhouse, I'm lucky to see anything. Ah, well"—she chucked the ball aside—"we'll just have to find ourselves another planet to spy on when that one's gone. Breaks my heart. Earth animals were just getting the hang of communication, too. If the Uprights don't bury themselves in polystyrene first, they'll fry in ultraviolet!"

Melba swallowed. Seeing the present in Boss Cat's crystal ball was a little like reading a choose-your-own-ending book. But what ending could be worse than extinction? She didn't like the one Boss Cat had planned for Melba-the-Robot, either, but she couldn't worry about everything.

"Tea time!" Boss Cat bellowed suddenly, scaring Melba out of her wits. As the Queen of Beasts tossed aside her turban and cloak, Melba felt her knees grow weak with panic. It was Melba-the-Robot's job to serve tea to her ladyship. Oh, brother! She herself didn't know the first thing about it.

Melba's eyes swung wildly around the tent. Maybe . . . if she could find some tea bags. But where was the kitchen? Boss Cat, ignoring the robot, began washing her hands and face in ordinary lion-fashion, noisily licking her paws with her pink tongue. Melba looked down at her own sweaty hands. "I could use a wash, too," she said, and—feeling desperate—began to lick the side of her hand.

When she heard the rattle of tea things behind the curtain, a big "Oh, good!" escaped her lips. Someone *else* was already back there making tea. But what if it was the real robot? Boss Cat hated to be tricked. She'd pulverize an impostor like her!

Melba wiped her hands on her jeans. How did she get herself into such messes, anyway?

Just in time, the curtains parted behind Boss Cat and a regular-size cat wearing a frilly white apron glided up to the table with a tray. On its face was a very worried expression. Melba was so relieved to see a cat instead of a robot, she broke into a smile.

"Two lumps of sugar," instructed Boss Cat imperiously, "and stir it if you don't want your ears chewed off."

"I'll have the same," Melba said, reaching out for a cup and saucer that nearly rattled away from each other before she had a good grip.

With paws as clumsy as they were shaky, the feline poured the catnip tea, then proceeded to serve three dainty salmon-cucumber sandwiches to each of them. "Whoops!" said Melba as one of Boss Cat's slid off the plate and onto the floor.

The serving cat whisked it back before Boss Cat even noticed.

Melba stared. There was something very familiar about that fuzzy face and that twitchy tail. Could it be? The cat locked eyes with Melba for the longest time as he stirred in her sugar cubes.

"Go ahead, you rotten little robot," said Boss Cat, guzzling her tea betweentimes. "Take a good look at your replacement. If Astrocat goofs up as royally serving me as he did spying, he'll be mummified along with you."

Having stuffed Melba's sandwiches into her mouth with her own, the gruffy lioness went right on trying to talk. "Mmmmmfff, mmmuumble. Who needs trouble?" *Chomp, chomp!* "Not someone in my exalted position."

Inside, Melba was doing handsprings. Astrocat! The animal in the ridiculous ruffles of a maid's uniform was none other than her friend, Super Spy. Imagine finding him here in the P.U. with Boss Cat. He knew who *she* was, she could tell, but, of course, he wouldn't let on.

Once he got behind Boss Cat's back, Astrocat made frantic signals to Melba. Pointing to the top of Her Majesty's head, he opened his mouth in a monstrous yawn, then let his own head loll on his chest.

Melba blinked. "Lovely tea," she murmured in a party voice.

After the second cup, Boss Cat's eyelids were heavy as stones. When her sinewy shoulders began to sag as well, she crumpled like a napkin and slid under the table.

Melba leaped to her feet. "Astrocat! What did you do to her?"

He gave her a purry hug around the legs, saying, "Have you forgotten my superspells?"

Bending down to hug him back, she could see more mischief in his eyes than anything else.

"You can take away a spy's credentials," he said with a dramatic gesture, "but you can't cancel his magic. I slipped a knockout spell in her tea."

"Great! Anyway," Melba said as Astrocat threw off his cap and apron, "I got your message. So where's Tommy? Much as I'd like to leave him here—"

"Later!" Astrocat grabbed her hand. "Right now the robot's being led to the hippo hunt. She needs us. Mostly, she needs you."

"You hunt hippos on Outpost Ouch?" Melba asked, trying to understand what he was saying.

Astrocat didn't answer. He was too busy shoving her out of the tent. "Superspells don't last forever," he hissed at her ear.

8

Escape to Danger

Melba had dozens of questions, but the mad escape from Boss Cat's tent didn't give her a chance to ask any of them.

In no time at all, she and Astrocat were back at the riverbank, beating a path through the reeds. "Stay close! The papyrus will hide us," he'd said before leaping on ahead.

The going was tough in such thin air. Finally, after pushing through rushes taller than she was, getting slapped and gouged and poked as she tried to keep Astrocat in sight, she called out for him to wait. "Can't we rest a minute? I'm not a cat, you know."

Astrocat braked and swung around. "Of course you're not. How thoughtless of me to expect a two-legged creature to keep up with one who has four."

59

Melba's chest was heaving as she wiped her face on the bottom of her T-shirt. "When are you taking me to Tommy?" she asked when she could. "That's what I'm here for, you know."

He didn't answer until he'd flattened a place in the reeds and flopped down. "Actually—" His eyes darted nervously as Melba made a spot for herself. "Actually, I, uh—"

The more he hesitated, the more she began to suspect things were not what they seemed. She'd seen that evasive spy look on his face before.

"Has something happened to Tommy?" she demanded, down on her knees beside him. "Tell me the truth now. Where is he?"

"Actually, Tommy isn't here. He never was."

"But . . . but you said! On my computer screen you said—"

"Subterfuge, mere subterfuge."

"Subterfuge!" shouted Melba, getting madder by the minute. "I don't even know what that means."

Throwing out his gleaming claws, he inspected them in the light. "Well, to put it simply . . . it means I fooled you."

"It means you lied! I've come all this way—" She lunged at Astrocat, intending to give him a good shaking, but he shrank out of range.

By then Melba was on her feet, hands on hips.

"You mean I didn't send Tommy to your planet? When I—"

"—When you cursed him into extinction? Hardly!" The fur along Astrocat's tail settled back into place. "The Earth's inhabitants are all endangered, and that includes Tommy. But I knew you wouldn't come without a good reason, so I made up the distress story. It was rather clever, if I do say so myself."

"Where'd he go, then? I couldn't find him anywhere."

"He was at your Video Arcade the last time I checked, waiting for Martin."

Astrocat continued to avoid her eyes, the way he sometimes did on Earth. She didn't know whether to believe him or not.

Suddenly he was up again, peering through the reeds behind them, his ears going like scanners. "Look," he said as he dropped to all fours, "we can't stay here. The robot's already in trouble you wouldn't believe."

Melba struggled to her feet, thinking, *I'm having a nightmare, but pretty soon I'll wake up and be in my own room and it will still be Friday.*

But she wasn't anywhere near her own room. She was off and running again, and she knew little more than she did before.

"So how come you have pyramids and pharaohs and stuff?" she shouted ahead to him now. "It's just like Egypt here! I don't get it. I don't get any of this!"

"The Queen of Beasts is a copycat, remember?" He flung the words over his shoulder as he bounced through the papyrus. "We animals in the queendom haven't had speech very long, which means we have no history—at least not a nifty ancient history like yours."

"But why Egypt?" Melba wanted to know.

Astrocat slowed to run beside her. "Who's the great breakthrough person? You! Naturally we monitor Morton Elementary. Boss Cat just decided we'd have an Egypt week like yours at school. She sometimes gets jealous of all the fun you're having."

A pawful of rushes slapped Melba in the face as he bounded ahead, but she heard him say, "Punch it! The robot will end up hippotized if we don't get to her before Eclipse."

None of it made sense to Melba. Not Boss Cat gazing into her gloomy crystal ball, or Tommy's whereabouts, or the robot getting *hippotized*, whatever that was. Overload and confusion were turning her brain to mush.

She was about to drop when she found herself following Astrocat up a tall palm tree, of all things. It was a date palm, she decided, having spotted the clusters of fruit under the leaves.

"See the dust clouds over there?" he shouted halfway up. "That means the camel race is over. We're just in time. The hippo hunt's next."

"I can't believe I'm doing this!" Melba muttered, digging into the shaggy trunk with her sneakers, reaching for another handhold, then pulling up and reaching again.

"Keep coming! Only a whisker farther," coaxed Astrocat. "You can see the whole game field from up here."

She didn't know what field he was talking about, but twice more she hitched herself higher and locked her legs around the trunk. At the top they grabbed on to fronds and Melba looked around. In one direction she could see the river snaking along. In the other she could see where the dense plant life petered out and the dunes took over.

Astrocat pointed to a tangle of low-growing vegetation that came up from the river. "That's where the hippo hunt takes place. See it?"

What Melba saw was a dozen or more trails meandering through the brush. From above, the broad area resembled a maze. She thought of wormwood. She decided the paths must be watering trails made by the animals.

Suddenly Astrocat's fur stood straight out. "There she is now. Oh, poor robot! They've just released her. That means the hunt's about to begin."

Sure enough, it was her double, Melba-the-Robot,

wearing jeans and T-shirt, unmistakable with that strawstack-yellow hair. She was walking toward the crazy game field. She was alone and she looked scared. Even from a distance, Melba could tell she was scared.

Melba's stomach did somersaults when she shifted to the other side of the trunk and saw a herd of restless hippos tramping around on a sandbar. When they showed their tusks to each other, their pink mouths looked big as caves.

"You mean Melba-the-Robot has to hunt those four-ton hippopotamuses?" Melba screeched. "She's a copy of me, remember? She won't want to do that."

"No, no, no!" Astrocat said, impatient as ever. "You've got it backward. The hippos are hunting her."

"She won't stand a chance!" Melba screeched again.

"That's why you're here. I'm a language and spying expert, you're the one with the brains. You have to save her."

"I don't get it. I thought you guys . . . the eagles said—"

"Never mind what they said. We've picked up some terrible habits from monitoring Earth. Barbaric habits! When Boss Cat discovered the robot had a mind of her own . . . well, robots aren't supposed to think for themselves, you know, so she got picked. *Designated,* you might say."

"But Boss Cat said she was being 'preserved' for scientific study. Why the pyramid, then, and the sarcophagus?"

"Sport first, burial next!" he said in a voice squeaky with fear. "The idea sets my teeth on edge. See that purple pavilion where the spectators are gathering? Boss Cat's supposed to be in it. The hippo hunt's been billed as the biggest sports event of Egypt week. I'm a mummy myself if she finds out I used a superspell on her!

"Here they come!" he cried, his eyes like moons, his tail vibrating. "They're starting up from the river. Quick, think of something! If she gets hippotized, it's the end, the very end!" He pushed his face into the hairy trunk, sobbing, "I've come to love her, don't you know?"

Instantly Melba gave her brain a command. It was one she'd never used before. If only she could synergize her electrical energies with the robot's. If only the cloning process could be made to work in *reverse.*

Concentrating all her powers, she knew something was happening. She could feel it. She was becoming light—featherlight, light as air. The throbbing of drums sounded in her ears as her atoms, in centrifugal reversal, underwent radical conversion.

Suddenly, unexplainably, the fusion occurred. She

was Melba-the-Robot and the robot was Melba the Brain. She'd caused the impossible to happen!

The two of them were one and the same, in one body, as in the beginning before she was copied by the animals' engineers.

No longer in the tree with Astrocat, the original Melba found herself facing the maze of paths that cut through the impossible brush, weak with the exertion of what she'd just done. And terrified.

There were no drums in her ears now, only the pounding hooves of a dozen hippos bearing down on her.

9

The Mark of the Hippo

Her brain in a fever, Melba tried to remember what she knew about hippos. They were big. They could be fast. They loved swimming and mud-wallowing. Worst news for her: they could follow a scent anywhere. Best news: they were herbivorous.

But if they didn't eat other animals, why would they come after her?

For the fun of it! came the quick reply. Same as on Earth. People often hunted for the fun of it.

For the longest time, Melba just stood there, too frightened to move. Not a single idea came to mind. Finally, something clicked. The trails! They must be hippo trails. She knew from her encyclopedia that each hippo had its own private path. If she could find one that was overgrown—no longer used—she might get away.

67

Darting around like a quarterback, Melba checked out one trail after another. It was hopeless! They were *all* beaten down, all being used.

A quick glance toward the river and she wanted to cry. By now she could see the dark backs of the hippos heaving above the brush. She could hear them crashing through the undergrowth, grunting with excitement. They'd sniff her out, no matter what.

Bravely, Melba turned to face her attackers, her heart exploding right out of her chest. In seconds, she and Melba-the-Robot would be hippotized. It was a terrible word, now that she knew what it meant.

"Astrocat!" Her eyes searched the treetops. "Where are you?"

The lead hippo, head down on spotting her, changed direction and came thundering right at her. Melba scrunched shut her eyes, but the piglike ears and bulbous snout were just as terrifying inside her eyelids.

"My kingdom for a miracle!" she cried.

As if in answer, a strong gust of wind hit her from behind, nearly blowing her over. A low moaning sound rose to a shriek as the suddenly violent wind blasted Melba and everything in its path with sand. She staggered and ducked, but every inch that wasn't covered was stinging.

Hippos in front, a sandstorm in back! What chance did she have?

"I want to go home!" she wailed, but the wind only filled her mouth with grit.

In the end, acting on instinct, she threw herself down and covered her head. She couldn't see or hear them now. If they trampled her, she'd never know.

The herd itself was within handshaking distance when it was stopped by the wall of sand. Peeking through her fingers, she saw that the leather-sided hippos had been left reeling, too. Acting fast, she scuttled backward into the brush.

Her pulses were still setting a record, but for the moment, at least, the hippos weren't interested in her. They acted as if they'd lost scent and direction both—churning and snorting and climbing all over each other. Were they trying to get their backs to the wind?

What happened next blew Melba every which way. From somewhere, as if by signal, every hippo produced a pair of goggles. The wind was still whipping up desert sand, but among the herd, order had been restored.

Snap, thwap! They sat up and adjusted their straps.

Melba looked on, openmouthed. On Earth, she'd have had to pinch herself. The goggles were identical to the ones she used in her swimming lessons—the ones that had SPEEDO printed across the nose strap.

They were even the same pastel colors. How ridiculous they looked with their wide-set eyes under plastic bubbles!

Then she remembered that swimming goggles were terrible for seeing anywhere except underwater. If they couldn't see her . . . and if the storm had confused them about her scent . . .

Grabbing her chance, Melba crawled through the brush on her hands and knees until she was out of range. When she stumbled onto a trail that circled around *behind* the herd, she took off at a full run in the direction of the river. The storm continued to shriek, sandpapering her skin, but she was so glad to escape she hardly noticed.

Now and again, she'd stop, shield her glasses, and scour the treetops for Astrocat, but with the fan-shaped fronds being whipped about, she couldn't see much. No matter. If visibility was as bad from above as it was on the ground, he wouldn't see her, either.

At the riverbank, Melba crept into a sheltered place to catch her breath and wait out the storm. After such a close call, she also needed to think.

She'd try to find Astrocat first, then figure out how to get Melba-the-Robot into a body of her own. She hadn't the faintest idea about how or when she'd ever get back to Earth herself. Wish power wasn't everything.

Poking finger holes in the sand, Melba longed for her own home, where she felt loved and safe. If only she could see her dad and her dog! Or her own room, where eighteen posters decorated the walls, where her little bear, Boo Boo, sat waiting on the bed. She'd walk into the house and say, "Hi, folks! Hi, bedroom! Long time no see."

Sniffling, she figured she'd even be glad to see Tommy Lane again.

She was feeling so sad she barely noticed the crackling of twigs as a rear guard of hippos straggled right past her hiding place.

A little later, hurrying back toward the grove of palms, Melba heard a series of strange sounds that stiffened the hairs on her arms.

Crack, crackle, screeeeeeech!

She swung around. The path behind her was empty. Was she imagining things?

There! It was an electronic sound, like her dad's CB radio. And it seemed to be coming from a dense clump of saplings. She crept forward to a place where she could peek through the trunks.

"Oh, no, not again!"

Behind a screen of foliage, scarcely hidden, was an enormous cow hippo surrounded by several calves. She had a walkie-talkie at one ear and was busily sending a message. Or trying to.

Melba ducked out of sight.

"Come in, Hipster!" the mother hippo kept yelling into the mouthpiece. "Riverside reporting to Hipster Herd. The storm's over and I've spotted the robot." She reached out with a hoof and smacked two calves who were fighting.

"Anybody alive out there?" she tried again.

Melba could tell by the way she slumped against a tree that she was losing her cool. "Will one of you dodo birds get on the squawk box?"

Someone apparently came on at the other end.

"Of course this is Boss Cow, who do you think? Tracking quarry here. Spotted the robot at the river. She's heading north, but I lost her again."

Melba shrank into her socks.

"Yeah, yeah—" the hippo went on, as impatient as any mother doing two jobs. "No camouflage. She's still in jeans and a striped T-shirt with that logo on the front. . . . No, Clarence, use your head. It's one of *their* brands, not ours." She snorted "Teenagers!" under her breath.

The cow hippo listened for a minute and Melba could imagine her glowering at the calves who wouldn't behave.

"So we've had some technical difficulties due to the storm? So what? Gives everyone a chance to buy popcorn and visit the rest rooms. Stash your goggles now and get on with it. I repeat: the robot's heading north. Over and Outpost Ouch."

The mother hippo then went charging through the brush after the calves, who'd been bugging her while she was talking.

Melba sprang to her feet and took off running. Of course the hippos would be able to talk! Even the ants on this planet could handle language. Faced with her own extinction, she'd momentarily forgotten that the animals here had speech, technology, *and* their native cunning.

Melba ran as fast as she could, peering up one date palm after another, expecting to see Astrocat any minute. He wouldn't go off and leave her, would he? He was crazy about Melba-the-Robot. They'd been each other's "pets" from the beginning.

"Astrocat, where are you?" she called again and again.

Before long she realized she was going in circles. How frustrating! She stopped, grabbed a breath, and looked around. Maybe getting lost was part of the game—how was she supposed to know?

Suddenly *thwump!* Something horrible landed on her back, sending her sprawling.

Snake! she thought, rolling over and over, screaming, "Get off, get off!"

Panic ended when she discovered it was Astrocat who was clinging to her neck for dear life. She'd nearly squashed him. He'd dropped from his perch in the tree and scared her to death.

"Whatever are you doing scoovering about in the dirt?" he yowled, shaking himself smooth. "And where have you been? I'm a complete basket case worrying about you and the robot. Where is she?" His expression grew tense. "Oh, no! Please, no! Don't tell me, I can't bear it!"

"She's me!" Melba said with a grin. "Or, should I say, I'm she?" Giddy at finding Astrocat, she got to her feet and brushed off her jeans.

Astrocat's expression stayed grim. He didn't know what she was talking about.

Melba tried again. "What I mean is, we're one and the same. For now, at least, the robot and I are more identical than twins."

"Oh, my dear little Upright!" He wrung his paws. "I don't like the sound of that. Is the fusion permanent?"

"Look, we escaped, didn't we? We didn't get hippotized." She bent down and pulled up her socks. "Not yet. But the hunt isn't over. I heard Boss Cow on her walkie-talkie and they'd already tracked me to the river."

"We'll go back the way we came," said Astrocat, his whiskers trembling. "Through the papyrus. But look sharp. It's not Eclipse yet and Boss Cat will be fuming."

He started back up the trunk of the date palm tree. "Stay here while I grab some grub and look around. I haven't forgotten my spying techniques, you know, not for a second."

Even with an Upright's inferior sense of hearing, Melba knew the hippos were coming before Astro-cat did. She recognized their sounds. Overhead, busily bragging about his spying prowess, Astrocat's blabbing once again got in the way of his observing.

Melba glanced up. There wasn't time! They were too close! She could smell their swampy smell.

"They're here!" she screamed, rooted to the spot.

Three hippos broke through the undergrowth. Her eyes widened. They were calves, no doubt the very ones she'd spied on, the mischievous hippos who'd given their mother fits.

She'd never heard a hippopotamus laugh in her life, but she knew they were laughing, all of them. The biggest one, mouth gaping like the Grand Can-yon, lunged first.

"Wait!" she cried, turning away. "Let's talk!"

Expecting to be chomped to bits, she felt only a light bump and a brush of whiskers on her arm.

"You're 'It,' " giggled the hippo calf who'd beaten the others to her.

It! thought Melba. Like in tag?

Before she could blink, he'd pivoted and roared off into the brush.

"Can't catch meeee!" the smallest one chanted

before turning tail and disappearing. The third one, more timid than the others, simply spun around and took off.

"You've been hippotized!" screamed Astrocat from above, sounding exactly like a banshee. "And by mere babes. You've been marked. Oh, my darling robot, you and I are doomed for preservation. It's the end. Alas, what a magnificent mummy I'll make!"

Melba shivered. Hippotized! Was that what *hippotizing* meant? Not death, but being tagged? Unknowingly, she'd been playing the animals' version of an Upright game.

A morbid thought slammed into her head. Slaughtered deer on Earth were tagged after the hunt as well.

Listening now to Astrocat's pitiful wails, she knew he had spoken the truth. She'd been marked. *Designated,* as he'd said earlier. And he, the robot's favorite, was doomed as well. As far as she could tell, the mark of the hippo on this crazy planet meant mummification.

10

On the Night Barge

The pink sky was turning to charcoal by the time Melba and Astrocat neared the village again. It would soon be dark and they still hadn't found a place to hide.

"Take your pick," Astrocat said, his cheeks wrinkling as he tested the air. "The river or the reeds."

Some choice! Melba hadn't forgotten the pitch black of the planet during Eclipse *or* the crocodiles that swam in this river. Now more than ever, she wished she were home in her own bed.

They hadn't yet left the safety of the bulrushes when they came across a rickety old pier that even Astrocat didn't know was there. They climbed up to inspect it. The river slapped against the pilings, making what seemed an ominous sound. Clinging to each other, they made their way to the far end of the swaying pier.

"Can't we just stay here a minute," Melba asked, "and figure things out?"

"Of course," Astrocat answered, still hugging her leg in his great fear of water. "I'm counting on you and your splendid ideas."

"Oh, give me a break!" She steadied him to sit beside her. "My poor brain's had it."

Melba let her legs dangle over the edge and the two of them stared gloomily at the water.

Suddenly, shifting to avoid a patch of splinters, she noticed a funny lump in her jeans pockets and began to smile.

"Astrocat, guess what we forgot?" She pulled out a handful of the dates they'd gathered. "They're not exactly jelly beans, but they're ripe and yummy. Hey, we can have a party, like on my porch at home."

"Fugitives can't be fussy," he muttered. Swiftly he popped a date into his mouth and chomped down on the sweet fruit. In seconds he'd speared two more, forcing Melba to eat fast to get her share. The dates were soon gone, the pits at the bottom of the river.

Melba licked her fingers. "I could ask Boss Cat for political asylum, the way I did the first time, but it probably wouldn't work. She'd eat me alive if she knew I ruined the hippo hunt."

"But you're not just *you* anymore. I mean, Melba-the-Robot's a servant here. She belongs to us. I mean, like, she's our property."

Growing even more agitated, he added, "The way animals on Earth have become your property. They plow your fields, take part in your sports, provide you with wool, leather, insulin. Am I correct to say meat is still the chief ingredient in your"—his lips curled—"stews?"

Melba nodded, hoping the animals hadn't developed a taste for roast Upright since her last visit. The games they played here were rough enough. She couldn't imagine being salted and peppered for the stewpot.

Nervously she wiped her hands on her jeans and tried seeing across to the other side of the river. Somehow it seemed safer over there with the pyramids, but she wasn't about to trust a crocodile bridge in the dark.

A ripple rolled down Astrocat's back, which meant he was thinking, too. "If only we could get that stupid crystal ball away from Her Majesty."

"What good would that do?" Melba asked.

"She's so sure you Uprights are becoming extinct. She has committees monitoring Earth for everything—one for acid rain, one for pollution. She has chairbeasts for excess radiation, overpopulation, ozone depletion." He ticked them off on his claws. "The data all goes into *Today's Horror Show*. That's what she calls her crystal ball. Actually, it's a very sophisticated computer."

"Really?" Melba gasped. Imagine! A data-digesting crystal ball that could also simulate storms and greenhouse effects.

"Every day she puts on her Madam Misfortune outfit and consults that ball to see what new atrocity you Uprights have wrought on yourselves and your poor animals."

Melba nodded. "Then she really does plan to . . . uh, *preserve* Melba-the-Robot for science?"

"Oh, my, yes! And probably the robot's favorite pet—me!" His eyes grew watery. "In ancient Egypt the royal cats, gazelles, and monkeys got mummified whether they liked it or not."

Melba shivered in the chill air. "And now she's me and I'm she and—oh, it's all so complicated. What are we going to do?"

"It isn't fair!" Astrocat sprang to his feet and began to pace. "After all those years of spying! After demonstrating my language skills and my superb ability, after dazzling Outpost Ouch with exquisitely original jelly beans . . ."

His tail flogged the pier as he raved on. "After all that, I, the famous Super Spy, have been assigned to Her Majesty's Tea Service. What a chop! And I'll never get that tea stuff straight. Yesterday I squeezed lemon on her sandwiches and dropped parsley in her lap."

Melba stifled a snort. Then, "Hey," she said, sitting up straight, "let's find the echosonography machine they used for copying me in the first place. You could make a whole bunch of Melba robots."

"It's been down for months. Anemia or something."

Her head dropped onto her fists. "Okay, it was just a thought."

It was nearly dark now. Melba shivered, knowing they'd have to sleep on this old pier. She wouldn't want to be mucking about in the bulrushes now.

Thanks to his superior night vision, Astrocat saw the barge several minutes before Melba did. She was aware only that he'd stopped pacing and was staring upriver.

"What are you looking at?" she asked finally.

"The night barge. It's making a final trip downriver before Eclipse. Hear the music?"

She couldn't see or hear anything. Yet. And then she did. Tiny points of light began to appear in the distance. Flickering on and off, they were more like blips than beams. The music, when it reached her ears, was also strange—thin and reedy, but pleasant in its own way.

Astrocat swung around to face her. "We'll hail it. Boss Cat would never think of looking for us on the night barge."

"Are you sure?"

"Positive! She uses the royal barge. This one is for workers. By now it will be almost empty." He danced around, his whiskers twitching with glee. "Once again, little Upright, my brilliance astounds me."

Melba wasn't sure about the brilliance. It took both of them—her doing a Boots whistle with two fingers in her mouth and Astrocat yowling at the top of his lungs—to get the barge master to notice them.

When the long boat finally slid up to the pier and Melba got a better look, she nearly turned and fled. The crew was straight out of a nightmare.

Surrounding the barge, giant fireflies were dipping and flashing above the water—on and off, on and off, glowing white, then fading to nothing. A good dozen of them lighted the way. When one the size of Astrocat blinked in Melba's face, she ducked in terror, blinded for a moment. She jumped when another one flitted so close she could feel the air blasts from its wings.

"You think we should do this?" she cried, but already Astrocat was shoving her up the gangplank.

The musicians at the rear of the barge were mammoth crickets, resplendent as an orchestra in their glistening black shells. They sat on a raised platform, making music that swelled and waned like nothing she'd ever heard, even on a summer's night. Catching the magic, Melba smiled in spite of her fears.

Once Astrocat and she had settled themselves on a bench, she spotted the oarsmen. They were *in* the water, out in front of the boat and attached by lines. They, too, were oversize insects—all bigger than she was—and they were pulling the barge. She could see their bulgy eyes when the fireflies flashed.

"What are *they?*" she whispered to Astrocat, recalling a certain horror movie her dad wouldn't let her see.

"They're our water boatmen. Two of their legs are paddles, don't you know? You've seen them, little water bugs jetting around in your ponds."

Melba shuddered. The ones she'd seen didn't have eyes the size of baseballs!

About then a whistle trilled through the air—a long tone followed by two lower ones. They were taking off, Melba guessed.

Ahead of them, the dark form of the barge master stood at the prow chanting, "In . . . out! In . . . out!" The barge leaped forward. "Stroke, blokes, stroke!"

As the musicians tuned up for another song, Melba began to relax. She hadn't the slightest notion of where they were going, but for the first time since arriving on the planet, she felt safe. Plainly, the crew knew exactly what they were doing.

She glanced aside at Astrocat, whose eyes were as heavy as hers. He'd be asleep in minutes. A night ride down the "Nile" might turn out to be very peaceful indeed. She sighed and leaned against Astrocat, who was leaning against her.

Whoossssssh! Melba let out a yelp as something heavy dropped over the two of them, pinning them to the bench. A net! A scratchy rope net! Astrocat, his legs jerking wildly as he fought the rope, only tangled himself more.

"We've been netted!" he screeched at her ear. "Tagged and now netted. Oh, my darling, we're doomed!"

One flash of a firefly and Melba recognized the barge master, who had flung off her hood and stood towering over them. A terrifying roar removed any doubts she might have. They'd just been netted by Boss Cat, Queen of Beasts herself.

Melba's hopes plummeted. They were as good as mummies already.

11

Terror in the Temple

"We've reached the Causeway!" Astrocat said with a shudder. "The Temple's next. That's where it happens—in the body shop."

Melba clenched her teeth. They weren't going to make her into a mummy, not if she could help it. She gave an angry push to the net that imprisoned them, but the knotted rope only burned her skin.

Astrocat had long since become a shivering clump of feline fear. If her brain had slunk away as well, she and Melba-the-Robot were history. Ancient history, to be exact.

Then she heard the trilling notes of the barge master's whistle and knew something was about to happen. Boss Cat's dark figure loomed again at the prow, more imposing than ever with her hood up. "Avast!"

she ordered the water boatmen. "Heave to, me hearties!"

Abruptly, the boat changed direction. Melba fell against Astrocat, who clung to her arm for dear life. The barge slowed, then swung around. She felt a bump as they hit the jetty. She couldn't see much now that the fireflies had gone, but the lack of light didn't faze the insects at all.

Minutes later, Melba got a case of the willies as she was being freed from the net. It was a new experience, being tended by the kind of creatures one meets only in bad dreams.

Behind her, if she could believe her ears, the fur was flying. Astrocat had found his courage and was spitting like a cougar.

"Don't *do* that!" she heard him rage. "I hate being tied up."

She herself decided it would be best to cooperate. For now. She took deep breaths as she was tied with strips of cloth to a board the size of a narrow table. No one needed to explain mummy wrappings to her! Then the night creatures hoisted the boards to their backs and the terrifying trip began.

It was Astrocat's yowling that filled the air at first, but Melba soon began to hear music floating up from somewhere. It was clear as a flute, although the notes were doleful and in a minor key. She could also hear

crying . . . and moaning. What sad sounds! Had
somebody died?

Whoa! She tried to sit up. They wouldn't be
mourning Melba-the-Robot yet, would they? While
she was still alive?

Before long, they were indoors and passing through
strange, dimly lit rooms. Strapped to the board, she
could see little but ceilings. A tunnel of some sort
came next, probably the Causeway Astrocat had
mentioned.

As the sounds of mourning grew louder, distinct
words began to reach Melba's ears. It gave her a start
to realize the wailing was, indeed, for Melba-the-
Robot.

"Ooooooooh, you adorable royal slave!" came a
single voice.

"How we shall miss you, sweet yellow-haired
chiiiiiild!"

A chorus of other voices joined in: "We implore
you, dear spirit, come live here again."

The sounds of grieving spiraled and peaked. The
effect was positively goose-bumpy. *Poor us,* thought
Melba, *that we should come to such an end!*

Suddenly, without the least warning, a dreadful
roar echoed through the Causeway. Boss Cat! It
could only be Boss Cat. And then, silence. Mourning, music, everything stopped. What was happen-

ing? Melba lifted her head, but she couldn't see a thing.

"What kind of namby-pamby nonsense is this?" came Boss Cat's angry voice over a bullhorn.

Another roar and then, "Shape up, you loafing lounge lizards! You're being paid for this job. I've a notion to fire the lot of you. I want some tears, do you hear? And I want some *agony*. You're supposed to be *sad*, not *sick!*"

Melba listened, mouth agape. So the mourners were hired? Like actors. She'd read about the Egyptian mourners of old who put on a good show whether they knew the dead person or not.

When the wailers began again, the volume of their suffering was three times greater. What a performance! Astrocat himself was moved to join in, his shrill caterwauling rising above everyone else's. At least he was sincere.

Melba squeezed shut her eyes, wishing she could plug up her ears as well. Why had she come back to this frightening place? She might be smart at math and computers, but she was no escape artist.

"Tommy Lane!" She lifted her voice with the rest. "I'll hate you for this as long as I live. I wanted *you* to be extinct, not meeeeeee."

Once they arrived at the Temple—or was it the courtyard?—Melba could see again. The area where the procession stopped was lighted by eight blazing

torches, each mounted on a pillar. In the ring of
firelight and smoke, the insects lowered Melba and
Astrocat onto two frames the height of tables.

Melba pulled her arms into her sides, hoping they
wouldn't have to touch. She needn't have worried.
The long-legged creatures were the shyest of all the
planet folk she'd met. After untying the cloths, they
scurried away into the dark recesses beyond the
pillars.

First thing, Astrocat found his ear and gave himself
a good scratching. Melba sat up, too, and tucked in
her T-shirt. Craning around to get a peek at the
mourners, she jumped to see a mass of crocodiles
thrashing all over the courtyard. What a sight! Up
on their hind legs, beating their breasts, tails out of
control! The ones who weren't wailing through their
long snouts were throwing dust or sand over their
heads. Melba was convinced. Astrocat and she were
about to become has-beens.

"Oh, no," Astrocat groaned, pointing to a table.
"There's the embalming stuff!" Canopic jars, a heap
of cloth strips, and a basket of dried plants stood
waiting.

Melba clutched her stomach. Her nose had already
picked up the spicy smells, some that reminded her
of bath oil. On the other side of the court, however,
a steaming pot was giving off the most dreadful odor.

"O my soul, the glue pot!" Astrocat's brow

bunched up. "Can't a great breakthrough person like you *do* something?"

All at once, the mourning subsided—the mourners being plumb worn out as far as Melba could tell— and Boss Cat herself stalked across the courtyard. She stood before the mummies-to-be. Dramatically throwing back her cape, she raised the crystal ball in one paw, a jeweled staff in the other. She looked regal as anything.

Melba wondered if she should curtsy, but she was too scared to move. She could only swallow, and into a dry mouth, at that.

In four more steps, Boss Cat reached her magnificent chair, a piece of furniture fashioned from antlers, where she sat down. She arranged her cape, then swept the room with an imperial gaze. In priestlike tones, she instructed the mourners to step forward to pay their last respects.

From the smell of things, Melba decided the embalming part was coming up fast. Paying last respects, as far as she knew, meant saying good-bye.

With great ceremony, the only alligator there dipped into a vat marked CROCODILE TEARS, then sprinkled the company of reptiles until their cheeks were streaming. Single file, the grieving ten-footers crawled up to exchange farewells with Astrocat and Melba. Most were blubbering so hard she couldn't understand a word, but she followed Astrocat's lead.

"Thank you," she'd murmur, or "You're too kind," or "I appreciate that."

"I'll miss you, too," Astrocat sobbed more than once.

So long as she didn't have to touch the swampy crocodiles, Melba was able to stay in control. In fact, she found herself half enjoying being Melba-the-Robot, star of such a spectacular funerary event.

In the end, the only alligator, his head dripping with imitation tears, rose up on his hind legs and made a beeline for Melba. Braver than the others, he lunged onto the table and pushed his snout right into her face.

"Hold it!" she cried, drawing back. What was he doing, trying to kiss her?

"Smack, smack, smack!" He kissed the air instead, his mossy mouth a mere fraction from hers.

Pushing up her glasses to get a better look, Melba recognized the face. It was Gotcha! Gotcha Gator, who had once terrorized newcomers to the planet, before he'd stolen her calculator and become an orthodontist.

"Gotcha!" she blurted out, scooting as far away as she could. "How are you, anyway?"

Clickety-click-snort. A few precision snaps of his jaws revived all her old terror.

When he closed in again to examine her face, the shivers on her spine became warnings. Suppose he guessed who she was? Did he realize the Upright in front of him wasn't the robot? Maybe—she braced herself—maybe it would be safer just to kiss him and get it over with.

"Open up!" he ordered suddenly.

Her mouth flew open. He was no longer Gotcha, but Dr. Gotchur-Grin Gator. If he'd had on his dental gown, she'd have thought she was in for her regular checkup. He went "hmmmmm" a few times, then peered into her mouth and poked around with one claw.

"Just as I thought," he said in a scolding voice. "Malocclusion. Why haven't you been in to see me at the office?"

Melba shrugged. "I didn't think I needed braces yet."

"I could have done a lot for your smile, you know that, kid?" His eyes filled—with real tears this time. He looked more disappointed than sad as he backed away and joined the others. He was a changed alligator. But how had she managed to trick him into sending her home that first time?

Recalling how easy that escape had been, Melba felt an unexpected surge of brain power. Trickery! It worked before. Why not try it again?

All during "final respects," her eyes had kept returning to the crystal ball, which stood on a marble stand next to Boss Cat. Periodic flashes showed it was functioning—or "booted up," as she and her father would say. Now, her eyes narrowing, Melba measured the distance between the ball and herself. Could she risk stealing it?

Astrocat gave her a knowing look. Leaning toward him, she whispered, "Make a commotion. Anything. Get her attention away from that ball."

Agreeing with a "Meowrrrrr," Astrocat—like any serious runner—went through a series of quick stretches first. When the hairs of his neck bushed out like a fur piece, he screeched, "A mouse, Your Majesty! Inside your cape!"

He left the board elongated, landed *kerwhump*, and streaked across the stone floor like a missile. After the mouse.

In less time than it took her to squeal "Eeeeiiiii!" Boss Cat was up on the table in a cloud of linen cloths. Canopic jars scattered and crashed, spices flew everywhere. Dancing around like a Gypsy, her cape pulled up to her middle, Boss Cat continued to scream. "Porters, get rid of that antler chair! At once! I hate surprises."

"Then have another!" Melba shouted. By then she had the crystal ball in her hands and was standing spread-legged on her board. "Stay where you are," she threatened, the glass ball over her head, "or I'll smash this on the stones."

"Why, you pitiful little pipsqueak, whatever are

you doing?" It took all four paws for Boss Cat to untangle herself. There was nothing regal about her when she whined, "You bring that back. Right now!"

Astrocat, who had taken refuge behind Melba, was sassing, "Make me!" but Melba did the talking. "I don't want to be a mummy and neither does Astrocat. Either you free us or *Today's Horror Show* becomes glass for recycling."

"What a cheeky little robot!" Dropping down off the table, head lowered, she started menacingly toward Melba.

"I mean it!" Melba stood her ground. "If you want this super ball, you'll have to guarantee Astrocat and Melba-the-Robot their lives. And help me get home besides."

"You!" Boss Cat stopped in midstep. She looked confused. "You're giving me double vision with all this talk. How many of you are there?"

Just in time, Melba remembered her manners. "I'm Melba the Brain, Your Majesty." She curtsied low. "I'm the Upright you elevated to Honorary Beast not long ago, at your birthday banquet."

Boss Cat fell back in surprise. "Melba the Brain, don't tell me! From the profligate planet, Earth? Citizens, gentle beasts—" She motioned for the mourners and stretcher-bearers to come close. "Look who's here. We have a real, honest-to-goodness Upright in our midst. She's an original, all right, our one-and-only Honorary Beast."

Her paw flew to cover her mouth. "Oh, my, what if we'd . . . oh, how dreadful!"

"Dreadful is right," moaned Astrocat, peeking around Melba.

"But what a piece of luck!" Boss Cat continued. "You can carry back 'the Word.' Knowing what you know, you can save the planet from destruction!"

"I can sure try," Melba said, nodding vigorously. "I love my planet and all its wonders, the same way you love yours. Unoriginal as Outpost Ouch is, there's no place like home, huh?"

Boss Cat's face fell into a child's pout. "Drat! I did so want to have a pyramid with real relics in it. You spendthrifts have such a long, colorful history."

Suddenly, remembering the Golden Rule, Melba decided to share with Boss Cat the way she'd want to be shared with. "You could still have relics," she spoke up. "Do what we did at Morton School. Make up a bunch of mummy cases and paint 'em. It's really fun to have pretend mummies—" Her glance fell on the glue pot. "And they're not so smelly as the real ones."

By then Astrocat—sensing Boss Cat's change of mood—was busily gathering up linens and sweeping spices under the table with his tail. "Better a live tea caddy than a mummified cat," he muttered, always the practical one.

"If Your Highness and I could put our heads together," ventured Melba, "I bet we could set up my formulas on this terrific computer. I have an experiment about acid rain in mind. For our Future Fair, you know? I'd sure like to get home and start it."

"Hold it a minute." Boss Cat's yellow eyes became slits. "You mean, if I let you go, there'll be no more insubordination from that repulsive runt of a robot?"

"No, ma'am," Melba said with exaggerated respect.

"And I get to win the next hundred games of Trivial Conceits?"

"Easily."

"All *right*, give me four!" Boss Cat put out a paw and they slapped hands. "Come on, hop down now. With a little luck, we can exit you through the false door. That's where the robot's slippery soul was to come and go when she visited us for parties."

"Good thinking," exclaimed Melba, glad no one had asked exactly *where* the robot was at the moment.

Boss Cat and Melba then sat down on the cool stone floor, the glowing ball between them, and began to enter Melba's data. It didn't take long. Her father—she thought with a grin—would love having a go at microcircuits as sophisticated as these.

When everything was set, Boss Cat motioned for the other creatures to gather around. This time it was Melba the Brain saying good-bye. Such farewells! "Last respects" were pale as a rehearsal in comparison. Astrocat gave her a sweet lick on the ear, and Gotcha Gator cried so hard he collapsed. It took a slosh of crocodile tears to revive him.

When Melba was ready, Boss Cat placed her finger on the crystal ball "Escape" key. "Your brain power will do the rest," she said.

Astrocat's shouted "Watch out, Earth!" were the last words to reach her ears.

12

What Only
Boots Knows

The first Earth sound Melba heard was the ringing of the telephone. Though some part of her was still eighty light-years away on Outpost Ouch, she herself was standing on the most beautiful back porch in the universe. Her own! She was home again—lightheaded, a bit loopy, but happy beyond words.

Letting the screen door slam as she ran into the house, she caught the phone on the third ring. "Hello?" she answered eagerly.

"Who is this?" came a boy's voice.

"It's Melba."

"Melba . . . the brainless wonder?" A rude cackle came over the line when she didn't say anything. Tommy Lane! She'd know that laugh anywhere.

"What'd you want?" he asked. "My mom said you called a while ago."

A *while ago?* If he only knew!

"What time is it?" she blurted out.

"You called to ask me that?"

"No, of course not. I just wondered, you know, how you liked being in that mummy case so long."

"You called to ask me that?"

"You're starting to sound like a broken record."

"Was Jake mad 'cause I left?"

She pulled a stool up to the counter, her legs still trembly from the transmigration. "He wasn't exactly happy. How come you sneaked off?"

Tommy laughed again. "I thought it would be a good joke. Besides, I wanted to get some practice in on the Golden Ax. Good thing I did. I beat Martin six games out of ten. He owes me some tokens."

"Tommy, maybe you and I could go to the Video Arcade sometime. I've never been there—not even once."

Melba drew back from the phone. *Whaaaaat? Who said that?*

"Tommy," she squeaked into the mouthpiece, "I take that back. I didn't say that, honest!"

"Huh? Is someone there with you?" He sounded surprised at first, then said, "I'd never go with you anyway, who you kidding?"

"Well, look, I just got home myself and . . . we were all worried about you, that's all. I'm glad you're okay."

"Yeah? So maybe I'll see you Monday." *Click.*

Melba hung up, too, but her face continued to burn. What had made her say what she did? She wouldn't go to the Video Arcade with Tommy if he were the last Upright on Earth. No way!

She got up and walked to the refrigerator, telling herself she couldn't go on referring to people as Uprights. Not if she wanted to be like everyone else. Fitting in was tough enough already.

She poured a glass of milk and carried it around the corner to the living room. For the moment, she forgot about Tommy. All she could do was smile. Everything was in its same old place—the flowered sofa, the lamp, her dad's lounger. Their house was small and plain, but it was lots cozier than Boss Cat's old Mortuary Temple.

Glad to be home safe, she wondered if it would ever be possible to be "one of the kids" at Morton after all that had happened. She now had a big job on her hands. A mission, really. She couldn't go back on her promise.

Melba sighed as she slumped into her dad's lounger and drank her milk. That was the trouble: having the power also meant taking the responsibility. If you know what's happening, you have to *do* something, and saving the Earth was the biggest assignment anyone could have.

Just then her father, whistling as usual, came in

the front door, a paper under his arm and Boots at his heels. She was so glad to see him, she flew across the room, got his neck in a stranglehold, and hung on until he cried, "Enough, enough!" It was a game they played to test each other's hug power.

"I love you more than ever!" she told him.

She headed for Boots next, but the hairs on his back stood straight up. "Grrrrrrrr!" came a rumble from his throat.

"Boots! It's me!" She reached for him again, but he backed away so fast his hind legs smacked the door.

"For shame!" her dad scolded, sending Boots into a crouch, his tail between his legs. "Melba's your mama, why are you growling at her? Good dog, come here now."

Boots went right to her father and lifted his spotted head for a pat. From behind his legs, he stared out at Melba as if she were a stranger.

She shrugged and walked away, pretending it didn't matter, even though her feelings were hurt. Plain as day, Boots was telling her to back off.

Her dad went on to hang up his tweed jacket. "How was school today? Anything exciting happen?" He laid his car keys on the stereo and loosened his tie. "Better hit the sack early, kiddo, you look tired."

Melba grinned. Who wouldn't look tired? She went back to the kitchen to set the table, telling her dad about her winning essay and how radical it was to be encased in plaster-gauze. Even chattering away about school, however, the lessons of the crystal ball stayed uppermost in her mind.

Later, over burger and fries, she asked, "Dad, what can someone my age do to protect the Earth and its environment?"

He laid down his hamburger. "I thought you'd never ask."

He pretended to dig in his shirt pocket. "Now, where's my *Dictionary of Endangerments?* Let's see—"

Melba laughed. "I know we recycle everything, but isn't there other stuff a person can do?"

"Educate yourself," he said. "That comes first. Say, what happened to that acid rain experiment you were going to try? With tomatoes, wasn't it?"

"Yes, but the Future Fair's two months away. I mean, what can I do, like, right now, this minute?"

"Stop breathing, I suppose. That would save oxygen, cut down on CO_2." He gave his mustache a swipe with the napkin. "No, that's too drastic. How about following the rule of three: don't waste, don't litter, don't pollute?" He stopped to think before adding, with a chuckle, "And don't hang out with the boys that do! Now that you remind me, I think I'll ride my bike to work tomorrow."

"Hmmmmm," Melba mused. What she needed was a list of "do's," not "don'ts."

"Guess what?" she said next, completely out of the blue. "I think I'm getting a crush on Tommy Lane."

That made her father put down his salad fork. "You're *what?*"

Melba's own fork clattered to the table, she was so shocked. What made her say that? She hated Tommy with a pure white flame and she always would.

"He's nice." The words sailed out over her private panic. "And I'd like to invite him over to do homework sometime."

"Well—" Her dad looked as uncomfortable as he had studying price tags in Young Fashions. "I don't know. I'll have to think about that. But aren't you kind of young to be having a crush? And what does Tommy have to do with the environment?"

"Nothing," Melba stammered. "Forget it."

Hopping up, she carried her dishes to the sink and scraped her plate, her hands shaking like crazy. What was going on, anyway? She was embarrassing herself to death!

Boots. Where was he? She'd go talk to him. He was the best listener she knew. "Boooooots," she called after excusing herself, "where are you?"

She found him curled up on her bedroom rug, completely zonked. Or pretending to be zonked. She closed the door, then stretched out on the floor and put an arm over him.

"Wake up," she whispered at his ear, "I'm scared. Someone else's words are coming out of my mouth. I think something terrible happened to me on the planet."

He opened one eye. Then both, the whites growing big as he pulled away. Making pitiful whining sounds, he crawled so far under the bed she couldn't reach him. No amount of coaxing would bring him out.

He was still there after Melba's bath.

Was it the mark of the hippo? she wondered. There was no visible mark where she'd been hippotized—she'd checked—but Boots, for sure, knew something she didn't.

13

Breakthrough at the Video Arcade

Melba found herself acting really weird during social studies on Monday.

For nearly two hours, she and her committee had been decorating the mummy case. When it was finished, everyone gathered around to exclaim how beautiful it was with its jewel-bright birds and flowers and metallic gold necklaces. The queen's makeup was perfect, right down to separate eyelashes.

"Ours is better than Tommy's," the girls whispered among themselves. His group had finished in half the time and were now cutting blocks for the pyramid.

The royal headdress, especially, drew lots of compliments. It had been painted one strand at a time by Mary Belle, who'd sort of been in charge of Melba's head all along. The hair, a glistening black, "looks exactly like Isis's hair," Mary Belle kept insisting.

The committee had all gone off to clean brushes when Melba experienced a terrible urge to make the pharaoh's wife blond. After all, she'd been the model and her hair had never, ever been black.

Knowing there'd be trouble ahead, Melba nonetheless stirred up a jar of yellow paint and started in. She had half the job finished when Jake noticed what she was doing and hurried over to the table.

"Melba! The kings and queens were Egyptian. Have you forgotten what they looked like?"

"So?" she answered. "I want her to look like me. How come Mary Belle gets her way about everything?" She dipped into the yellow jar and kept on, painting faster than ever now that she was about to be stopped.

Jake didn't know what to say—she could tell by the way he just stood there scratching his beard. "Melba, my dear, this isn't like you. Please! Mary Belle's feelings will be hurt. Come now, no harm done. We'll let it dry, then paint it over tomorrow." He gave her a quick smile as he took away her brush.

Melba wiped her hands on a paper towel and returned to her desk—mortified! Who did she think she was? And what had made her pick up that yellow paintbrush in the first place? She would have jumped into the Nile River if she'd been able to.

When the others came back to the room and saw what she'd done, some very sour looks came her way.

"She *what?*" Mary Belle shouted as soon as Jake told her. Looking back at Melba, her eyes stabbing like daggers, she stalked off mad.

"I can't believe you!" Sandra said as she sailed past on her way to soothe Mary Belle.

Melba felt her lips quiver. Melba the Nice Little Mummy had become Melba the Monster, saying and doing things she'd only have thought about before. It was true, she had hoped the Egyptian queen might look a little like herself, but it was really obnoxious of her to insist.

When the final dismissal bell clanged, she jumped up and fled the room.

Outside in the hall, Melba fell into step behind Tommy and Martin, who got out just ahead of her. She hated having to face the kids on the bus, but tomorrow in class would be even worse. What had come over her?

In spite of her own misery, she couldn't help hearing the two boys arguing. Their voices got louder as they went along. Tommy wanted to go to the Video Arcade again. Martin didn't.

"Yeah, but you owe me," Tommy kept saying. "Your mom won't care. Come on, maybe you'll win your money back."

Martin kept shaking his head no. "I can't tonight, honest."

"If he won't go with you, I will," Melba called ahead to them. Without knowing why, she was suddenly taking long steps to catch up with Tommy.

"Yeah, good idea," said Martin, looking relieved as he stopped off at the water cooler. "Go with her. I'm broke, anyway."

Melba's mouth was drier than Martin's. Why had she said that? She was too good at games. She'd beat him, and then he'd hate her even more.

"Hey, Melba, you mean it?" A grin appeared on Tommy's freckled face. "You got some money on you?"

"Would I say I'd go otherwise?" Sure enough, she had two dollars from Saturday's allowance, right there in her jeans pocket.

"All *right!*" he said. "But kind of walk behind me until we get outside, okay? Guys . . . you know, they'll think we . . ." The pink in his cheeks gave him away.

Oh, yuk! thought Melba. *He thinks I like him.*

"I don't mind," she said with a sniff, "if you want to be like that." What she was thinking was, *One game and I'll sneak away. This isn't me, missing the bus to go to the arcade, I just know it isn't.*

Things were hopping by the time they reached the mall video parlor. A bunch of junior high kids, out earlier, were there ahead of them, so only two games were open. Tommy shrugged, saying he could play anything.

Melba hung back, dazzled by the noise and the machines, but excited, too. Tommy pushed up to the token changer and fed it a dollar. Melba followed with one of hers. She felt a little out of it, with Pac-Man being the only game she'd ever played.

"Way to go, Melba," someone said as she passed. She looked around to see Kevin nod from a console. Then he and Josh went back to zapping spaceships or enemies or whatever it was they were zapping.

Tommy said he liked the quest games best, so they cruised around until they found one. At first, Melba just watched. When she had the chance to play, she discovered she was a total disaster. She pushed the joy stick up when she should have pushed down. Twice she fried herself on the flames and let the drug dealers go free. She never got a single bonus. At the end of two games she was ready to quit.

For once, Tommy was patient. "Come on, you need to start with something easier."

He went around the arcade with her until he found a game called Wonder Boy and said they'd take turns. Even there she was a failure. Tommy's points were way above five thousand, so he was the one who got to display his initials on the winners' board.

"Tommy, what's happening?" she gasped as the

graphics background on the next game did a switcheroo.

"You just warped, dummy! Now you're in the meadow, but you still have to get those guys with the Mohawks."

When Melba's money ran out she had to quit, but Tommy gallantly offered to buy her a soft ice cream at the snack bar. Melba was flabbergasted. He hadn't been this nice since first grade.

Waiting at the ice cream machine, it was clearly Melba's *other* voice that piped up and said, "Tommy, you're really fantastic at video games. I'm so impressed I can hardly stand it."

"Thanks," he mumbled, turning away.

She pressed her lips together, as if that would keep them in line. Either her brain had warped or she was becoming a split personality.

Outside the mall, Tommy simply said "Bye" and took off, leaving Melba to get home by herself. She shrugged and started out, licking her ice cream and wishing she had better hand/eye coordination. Tommy said that's what it took.

"He's not so bad, once you get to know him."

Melba nearly left the sidewalk. *She* didn't say that! She was eating ice cream.

"Am I going nuts?" she asked, looking over her shoulder.

There was giggling from somewhere. "I made you

forget about me, but now you have to remember. Isn't there something familiar about my voice?"

"It sounds like me, but it doesn't. It's like hearing myself on a tape recorder." Melba stopped and took a sharp breath. "Am I having this conversation with . . . Melba-the-Robot? I thought you stayed on the planet."

"When I had a chance to piggyback to Earth? No way. I had too much fun last time. I won't go back until your wishing sends me back."

"Wish power, that's it! You've been saying and doing all the things I wished I could, haven't you. Just like before."

"Pretty weird, huh?" came the voice of the robot. "I'm sorry I got you in trouble at school, but you did bring it on yourself, you know. Being jealous of Mary Belle."

"But what about Tommy?" Melba asked, hurrying on so no one would catch her talking to herself. "You're the one who likes Tommy, not me."

Another giggle, and then, "We both do."

"Ugh! You've blown a circuit if you think that."

"Come on, admit you like him a little. I know you wish he liked you a little."

Melba kicked through somebody's leaf pile, feeling her face grow warm. "I think I'm going to wish you were back on Outpost Ouch. Boss Cat will have a fit. Astrocat's totally random when it comes to tea service."

"No, no, wait! You saved me on the planet, now I want to help you. How else will I visit Morton Elementary if it isn't there someday? If it melts down or blows up or washes away with warm tidal waters? Remember what you promised Boss Cat."

"Of course. How could I forget?"

"I can help you," Melba-the-Robot pleaded, "really I can. Give me one school day. Please! I'm brainy, just like you, and I care about what happens to the Earth. You won't be sorry, honest."

"Well, it wouldn't be so bad if I could control—"

"—The wishes, right? At the moment, you're wishing we didn't have to share the same body and voice, so I'm going to leave."

Melba stopped short. "But will I get to see you? And what if I miss you too much?" she asked to be polite.

"You'll see me later," came a last whisper, "but not now. Love . . . your duplicate."

The separation, unlike the fusion, was painless.

Melba looked around in all directions, desperately wanting a glimpse of her double, but no one was there.

Flashing back to Outpost Ouch, Melba remembered growing lighter than air. She remembered her pulse drumming in her ears and how terrified she'd been. This time, she simply *knew* the robot was gone. They were separate entities again. She, the original, was alone in mind and body both.

Boots knew it, too. When she got home, he jumped all over her, licking her hands, whining with delight to have his one-and-only Melba back.

"Would you like dinner early?" she asked after the two of them had a good tumble on the floor.

"Broof!" said Boots, his tail going like a propeller.

Two minutes later, Melba was on the phone.

"I have to go to the library tonight," she told Kim. "I need to look up some stuff about acid rain. Want to go with me?"

After Kim said yes and they'd made plans, Melba found enough courage to say, "I think everyone in social studies hates me. I'm glad you don't."

"Of course I don't. I tried to catch you after class today, but you left too fast."

"I don't know what got into me," Melba said feebly, all the while knowing exactly what had gotten into her.

Kim's laugh bubbled through the phone. "Mary Belle had it coming, the way she was acting. Hey, meet you on the corner at seven. If I don't practice, Mom says she'll give my clarinet to the homeless."

Melba laughed, too. "Okay. See you."

Melba hung up and leaned against the wall. Maybe things would be all right. With one good friend, Kim, and one "iffy" friend, Tommy, she might actually get through the next day at school.

14

The Trouble
with Robots

The next morning Melba was wakened by sniffing sounds. She rolled over, too sleepy to investigate, but the sniffing went on. At last she sat up. It was Boots, standing in front of her closet, his nose taking inventory of its contents.

"Hey, Boots, what's in there?" She threw back the covers. "Do you smell an old sandwich?"

She walked across the room, slid open the closet door, and leaped a mile. There, sitting cross-legged on the floor, was Melba-the-Robot.

"What are you doing here?" Melba asked after muzzling Boots and shoving him out in the hall.

"I've been thinking—" the robot said as she stood up.

"Me, too, and I'm not so sure this is going to work."

115

"You and I shouldn't dress the same today. And we mustn't be in the same place at the same time."

"You know, you could have knocked!"

The robot didn't answer. She was too busy sliding hangers along the rod. "Here"—she tossed Melba a pair of jeans—"you wear these. I found a skirt and jacket I like. Oooh, cute! I just love all the Earth slogans on this denim jacket."

"Me, too," Melba said under her breath.

Happy as a shopper with a credit card, the robot stripped Melba's favorite new things off the hangers and went on talking. "I should be the one who rides the bus, don't you think? I've never done that. You can ride with your dad."

Melba stalked out to dress in the bathroom, nearly tripping over Boots, who was cowering under the sink. "She'd better not use my toothbrush," she muttered, hiding it at the back of a drawer.

As things turned out, Melba didn't see the robot again until she got to school. It was plenty embarrassing riding all the way to Morton on her dad's handlebars, even though he dropped her a block away, but she made it with five minutes to spare. It was the rest of the day she was worried about.

Everyone was off the buses and inside when she arrived. All except one girl in a cute denim jacket. She and the driver were out looking under the bus, and Mr. Garrett was gesturing like mad.

Melba did a double take. *Oh, no!*

"I'd like to see your latest emission test for this bus," the robot was insisting in a bossy voice. "Black smoke was billowing out of that exhaust the whole way."

Melba cringed and hurried on into the building. She should have stayed home with a stomachache. Before the day was over, she'd need the paramedics! How many times had she wanted to report bus number 17 for violating emission standards? She'd never had the nerve.

Keeping her eyes lowered, Melba hurried on to first-period math in Miss Flowers's room. She passed kids who gave her a cheery "Hi, Melba" or "Hi!" Maybe they'd forgotten what she did yesterday. Mary Belle wouldn't look at her, of course, but what could she expect?

Halfway through class, with the other students working math problems at the board and Melba concentrating on her advanced calculus, a girl came into the room carrying a note.

"Melba," Miss Flowers sang out, "it's for you. The principal wants to see you in his office. Right now."

Everyone turned to stare. *Thanks a bunch, Miss Flowers!* What had that robot done now?

Melba left the room with her heart pounding. There was no way to explain that she had a double who was running around school *doing* things. He wouldn't believe she had a clone. Even the word "android" mightn't register if he didn't read science fiction. She couldn't say, "Mr. Miller, she's actually not a computer-driven robot, the kind you're used to seeing in the movies." None of it would make sense to the average Upright.

There I go again, thinking Upright.

By the time she walked into the principal's office, she'd resigned herself to taking the rap—whatever it was.

"Hello there, Melba." Mr. Miller shook her hand, then nodded toward a chair beside his desk. "Sit down, please."

She sat down, glancing at the family pictures on his wall. Maybe he had a little girl at home and would be nice. She put a big smile on her face, but her fingers were twisting the hem of her T-shirt.

"I read the note you left for me," he began. "I'm quite excited, to tell you the truth, to know you've taken such an interest."

Melba nodded. *What note? What interest?*

"I have a feeling this preys on your mind. You worry a lot about it, don't you?"

She nodded again. She worried about everything.

"Yes. Well—" Mr. Miller sorted through some papers on his desk. "Somewhere here I have a request from the PTA and a letter from a patron, both expressing the same concern. Both letters asked, 'Can't the school community do something to help?' "

Melba jumped at the chance to make sense. "I bet they could." It occurred to her that facing the principal wasn't a whole lot easier than facing Boss Cat.

"Here it is." He held up a letter. "The PTA has some money to spend. They want to fund some kind of clean-up drive." He located the second one. "And the parent who wrote this thinks our grounds are a disgrace."

"I agree . . ." Melba ventured. "The grounds are a disgrace. And so's the cafeteria when the kids don't like what's for lunch."

"Melba"—Mr. Miller sat forward—"how would you like to be our student coordinator?"

"Our what?" Egyptian hieroglyphics were clearer to her than this conversation.

"You'd be our idea person as well as a go-between for the student body and the PTA. I'm as worried as the next person about what's happening to our *global* environment, but cleaning up one's act, in my opinion, starts at home. I'd like you to be the student leader of a clean-up campaign."

Melba brightened at once. She couldn't believe her ears.

"Well, the clock's certainly ticking," she said, borrowing something her dad said a lot.

They talked some more, and the principal mentioned things they could do, like planting trees to use up excess CO_2 or having an "end litter" campaign to teach consideration for the Earth.

When he asked, "Any ideas?" Melba leaned forward to say, "We could call our campaign 'Adopt-a-Playground' for little kids and 'Adopt-a-Campus' for us big ones. My dad and I have already adopted a whale, as well as a highway where he grew up in Nebraska. It's neat, adopting stuff." She didn't tell him she'd just adopted a planet.

They talked about slogans and T-shirts and maybe a big musical rally to kick things off. When Melba suggested they set up Dumpsters and start their own recycling program right there at good old Morton, Mr. Miller smacked his desk and said, "Wonderful! Let's do it!"

"We could have contests to see which class would bring the most aluminum or plastic"—Melba's hands were now going as fast as her tongue—"and the winners would get to paint animal faces on the Dumpsters."

"You mean, like a reward activity?" he asked.

"Sure. They could choose endangered species—there are jillions!—and paint heads of those animals all over the Dumpsters." Melba was definitely into painting of late. "No lie, kids would love it!"

She got so excited she didn't want to leave. When the phone lit up, however, she knew she had to.

When Mr. Miller stood, they thanked each other and he said they'd talk again, later in the week. "Soon, anyway. With that clock ticking away, we can't fool around, can we?"

"No, sir!" she answered.

Melba's feet hardly touched the floor on the way back to class. Her head was already full of slogans. "Waste the Wasters" would be a good one for the cafeteria. They could have T-shirts that said "Trash Makes Cents, Recycled" or bumper stickers: GLOBAL RELEAF—PLANT A TREE. She could imagine the mountain of recyclables if every kid took part. And think of all the trade-in money the school would get out of it.

Cutting through the courtyard to save steps, Melba was suddenly forced to duck behind a hedgerow. Her look-alike had cornered their biggest sixth-grader right there by the drinking fountain—Greg Horton, who looked as if he might sprout a mustache any day.

"If you don't pick up that gum wrapper," the robot yelled, "I'm going to make a citizen's arrest!"

"You and who else?" he yelled back, pushing his face right down to hers. "I'm really scared, you know that? I'm just shakin' all over."

The robot whisked a notepad out of her pocket, an orange spiral Melba recognized, and went stomping off after Greg. "Litterbug! I want your name and social security number," she shouted at his back, "and I want you to promise never again—"

Melba hurried off the way she came. "That's not the way to go about it," she said under her breath. "You're going to ruin everything."

By lunch hour she was a wreck, wondering what was going on behind her back and in her name. They should have planned things better.

Knowing the two of them couldn't be seen in the cafeteria together, Melba slipped out to the 7-Eleven on the corner for a Slurpee and a hot dog. Her heart took a dive when she walked in and saw who was there ahead of her. In a loud voice, the robot was now lecturing the management, a gray-haired lady who'd run the store for ages.

"So where's your recycling bin, anyway?" she demanded. "And what about those plastic bags you use? Are they the biodegradable kind?"

Melba wasn't surprised. She'd wondered the same things. But the robot hadn't grown up in the Upright culture and didn't understand that "messy but well-meaning" was just the way most people were.

After paying, Melba took the robot's arm and steered her toward the door. "Come on, you can have half of this. We better talk."

The drawer of the cash register slammed shut behind them. "That twin of yours could sure use some tact lessons," the lady growled at Melba.

"Yes, ma'am, that's what I think."

Their faces were both plenty red by the time Melba got her double outside, but the robot wasn't finished. "Tact?" she screamed. "How can she talk about tact when the planet is having an ecological crisis? Are all you Uprights so dense? Doesn't anybody care?"

Melba puffed out her cheeks as she unwrapped her hot dog, wishing the robot was anywhere else but standing there waiting for half her lunch. When she looked up, her double was gone.

Hurrying back to class, Melba told herself the robot was only trying to help. And did help, in one way. She herself would never have been so bold as to ask the principal for a private talk. So how could she have been so ungrateful? One mighty blast of wish power—and *whoosh!* She'd sent her back to the planet. Or sent her somewhere. And they hadn't even said good-bye.

Would Boss Cat think she hadn't kept her word, that she didn't care any more about Earth's future than the kid with the gum wrapper or the 7-Eleven lady?

Melba was relieved, walking into social studies, to see the queen on the mummy case had black hair again. Jake must have painted it himself, to be nice and save her embarrassment. She was a model student the rest of the period. Though she'd always craved getting a "Needs improvement" note, she didn't want one from him.

It was close to dismissal time when Jake reminded the class that they needed to choose projects for the upcoming Future Fair.

"Only eight people have put their names on the sign-up sheet. And some of these sound like very big undertakings. Carla, the video you want to make on twenty-first-century sports . . . want to team up with someone?"

Three hands shot in the air—all boys. Carla, who was hot at baseball and basketball both, took her time, but finally chose Pete to be her teammate.

Jake wrote down his name and thanked them both.

Becky and Nanci decided next that they'd work together on designing tomorrow's kitchens. A minute later, Samuel volunteered to help Martin do a project on the future of simulators.

"Melba?" Jake looked up from the clipboard. "An experiment demonstrating the effects of acid rain sounds pretty heavy. How do you plan to set that up, anyway?"

She sat forward. "With two control groups of tomato plants and a growing light. I'll have to collect rainwater, then I will add minute amounts—I figured it out to be twenty drops per gallon—of sulfuric acid. That's the ratio they're finding in some industrial—"

"Pardon me, but sulfuric acid? Where will you get that?"

"Out of my dad's car battery."

There was suppressed laughter around the room.

"Acid's dangerous," she added quickly, "but he says he'll supervise that part."

"Sounds solid. Think you could use some help?" the teacher asked.

"Okay." She crossed her fingers under her desk. Kids didn't usually pick her. After yesterday, who would want her for a partner?

The room grew quiet as a burial chamber as kids looked at each other.

Then, "Put me down," said Tommy to gasps of surprise. "Sulfuric acid! Man, I like the sound of that one."

"Great," said Jake, "we'll expect big things."

"But smallish tomatoes," quipped Melba, making everyone laugh.

Melba herself grinned as she scooted down in her desk. She hardly knew what to think. Tommy . . . choosing her!

A few minutes later, boarding bus number 17, she nearly blew it. She'd just started up the aisle when she saw her double sitting near the back, looking at her with frantic eyes. "No!" she seemed to say. "You can't! *I'm* here."

Melba whirled around and got off again, acting

as if she'd forgotten something. Now she was really confused. "One school day"—wasn't that what the robot had said?

She didn't mind walking the two and a half miles home. That was easy. What bothered her most was that the robot was sitting next to Tommy. And he looked very happy about it!

15

What on Earth!

"Boots, I'm home!" shouted Melba. She was still thinking about Tommy—he'd be terminal if he had to sit next to *her*!—but she couldn't be mad at him, not now that they were partners. Anyway, the crunchy leaves and Halloween smells on the walk home had put her in a terrific mood.

She'd hardly closed the back door when Boots came skidding across the kitchen floor, a wild look in his eyes. On seeing Melba he bristled, funneled up his cheeks, and howled.

"What's the matter?" she cried, tossing her book bag. "Don't you like me anymore? I like you."

His tail drooped, but he finally crept close enough for a hug.

"That's better. Have I been too busy lately to fix

127

you a nice dinner? Come on, it's time I paid some
attention to you."

Melba went straight to the refrigerator. She found
the dog food can on the top shelf, but it was empty.
What's more, there was a spoon in it. Who'd feed
her dog and leave an empty can in the fridge? She
rinsed the can at the sink and chucked it into the
recycling bag.

When she bent down for Boots's water dish, she
saw it had already been filled. What's more, there
was a pink chrysanthemum floating on the fresh
water. Melba laughed. A flower in the dog dish!

Still chuckling, she went on to change her clothes.
Her dad might do something like that, just to be
funny, but he never fed Boots. That was her job.

The mystery was solved when she reached her
room and found her jacket and skirt spread neatly on
the bed. Suddenly everything made sense, including
Boots's weird behavior. *She* had been there!

Melba stood listening for a minute. Maybe the
robot was still in the house, waiting to say "good-
bye" or "good luck." But if she was, Boots would be
doing more than just slinking around.

Melba padded down the hall in her stocking feet
and pushed open the bathroom door. No one there.

The computer den next. If the robot was anywhere, she'd be at the computer; at least, that's
where Melba would be. But the den was empty and

the computer was cold. The robot had kept her word. "One school day," she'd said. No doubt she was already eighty light-years away on Outpost Ouch. With the animals' technology, interplanetary travel was a breeze.

Melba went back to her room, where she changed into her best raggy jeans. The house was so quiet she could hear Boots slurping water in the kitchen. She'd be lonesome for a while. What would it have hurt to let the robot stay the rest of the week? How could she have passed up a chance to go to school half time while her double went the other half?

Before hanging up her new jacket, Melba tried it on and studied herself in the mirror. The robot looked cuter in denim than she did, she was pretty sure. Turning slowly, she struck a model's pose, her hands in her pockets. That was when she found the folded paper with her name on it.

A note! Melba dropped onto the side of the bed.

"Call me after school," said the scrawly handwriting. Her heart did a skip-to-my-Lou when she saw the initials T.L. at the bottom.

Melba stared at the note a very long time. Had Tommy written it and slipped it into the robot's pocket on the bus? Or had her double planted it there herself, a last joke from the wish giver?

She'd never know if she didn't pick up the phone and call.

"Tommy, is that you?" she asked a few minutes later.

"Who'd you think, my twin brother?"

"Don't mention twins!" Melba said with a laugh. Then, quickly, "I found a note in my pocket that said I should call you."

"Oh, yeah? Hey, can you hang on a second while I get my potato chips?"

Melba made a face. When he came back to the phone she said, "Hold on while I pour myself some juice, would you?"

She could hear him whistling, then singing, then tapping the phone. This was some conversation they were having.

"All right," she said, back again.

"So . . ."

"So what did you want?"

"It's about the acid rain thing. I had an idea. My uncle owns a greenhouse close to Morton. We could grow the tomatoes in there, I'll bet, if I asked him. You want me to?"

"Hey, that would be perfect. Better than in the basement on our windowsill."

"He's a neat guy. He raises goats and lets me feed the newborns sometimes."

She heard the savory crunch of potato chips going down, so she took a drink of juice. A long silence followed. Finally, grinning at the mouthpiece, Melba said, "Call me if you ever want to go play video games again."

That time it wasn't the robot speaking. It was Melba herself.

"I'll think about it. Maybe tomorrow, huh?"

"Maybe. Wish I could play better. I'm not very good."

"You're good enough. You buy the ice cream this time, okay?"

"Okay." *Same old Tommy!*

After they hung up, Melba headed straight for the computer. The sooner she nailed down her calculations for the sulfuric acid solution, the sooner they could get started. Tomatoes don't grow from seed overnight, especially the poor plants they were about to subject to acid rainwater. Actually, she felt a bit sorry for them, but in the name of science . . .

The computer hummed to life, filling the room with its cozy noise.

All of a sudden, the phrase "in the name of science" gave Melba the chills. The ancient Egyptian mummies were doubtless preserved in the name of religion, but Boss Cat's ideas were more modern. To think she herself—mistaken for the robot—might have been a mummy for the sake of science!

Melba named her file ACIDRAIN, then waited for the computer to digest the information. Having thought of Outpost Ouch, she now crossed her fingers for Melba-the-Robot. She hoped there wouldn't be any trouble, that she could go back to her old life on the planet. She wished the same for Astrocat, too, who was so endearing in spite of his wily ways. Melba knew she'd keep her end of the bargain. She'd do her utmost to preserve the planet that had always supported her.

Suddenly the screen of her P.C. began to flash. Melba frowned. Was she getting an alert? A perfect white circle burned into the screen, something that couldn't happen on her machine without a graphics board. *Her* letters were amber.

A smaller circle appeared inside the larger one. Puzzled, Melba drew back and watched a ring of letters join to become words between the two circles.

"What on Earth!" she exclaimed.

Right in the center, looking a little like the MGM lion, but crowned with Madam Misfortune's turban, was Boss Cat. She didn't roar or anything. She just sat there on the screen looking regal. The letters, when they quit dancing, spelled SEAL OF APPROVAL at the top and COURTESY OF OUTPOST OUCH at the bottom.

Melba couldn't stop grinning. Somewhere on the Animals' Planet, a modem capable of reaching Earth was bringing her an A-OK.

Her fingers flew back to the keyboard. She pressed "Save," flipped on the printer switch, answered the questions, and hit "Print." She swung around to face the printer, only to see the blank paper roll up . . . and remain blank. Her SEAL OF APPROVAL had appeared and disappeared as neatly as a warp in a video game. Once again ACIDRAIN was the file heading at the top of the screen.

Melba sat openmouthed. Unbelievable! But she'd been contacted twice now—she *had* to believe. With a direct hookup to Boss Cat's amazing crystal ball, anything could happen. Anything! She might even appear on *Today's Horror Show* as a guest sometime. What would that be like?

Staring outside where October leaves were falling like rain, Melba leaned back and let her imagination have its way.

It was Astrocat who floated into her line of vision first. He carried a mike in one paw. He appeared to be doing some kind of interview.

"We're here at beautiful Morton Elementary on a sunny afternoon," she could hear him say. "The Future Fair is now under way, with crowds of excited visitors milling about."

He approached Melba, who looked smashing in her pink jeans and Trash-a-Thon T-shirt.

"Excuse me, miss, but what are these scrawny yellow plants you're exhibiting? My, but they look pitiful."

"Those are tomatoes. Tommy and I grew them with acid rainwater in a greenhouse environment. They do look sick, don't they?"

"Tell me, why did you choose to do an acid rain experiment when you might have teamed up with Mary Belle over there? Look at those far-out hairstyles she's demonstrating."

"Hmmmmm," she answered. "The truth is, I couldn't quit thinking about mummies. During Egypt week, I realized how much the ancient Egyptians cared about life. They wanted to go on living forever."

"So—you Uprights had better clean up your act if you want your species to live forever. Is that the idea?"

"Well, yes and no. It's the Earth we want to live forever. Dynasties come and go. Plants and animals have to take turns, too. But the Earth has a future to match its past if we Uprights will only take care of it. Acid rain is only one problem of many, but that's where I decided to start."

Just then Boots came into the room and plopped down at her feet, abruptly ending the interview. He gave Melba an adoring look, and his tail thump-thump-thumped against her leg. She reached down to scratch his ears.

"Good dog. You're smarter than some people,

aren't you? You were recycling bones a long time ago."

"Broof," said Boots before his eyelids slammed shut. Melba had to laugh. He was a great one for conserving energy too.

CELEBRATING
YEARLING
25 YEARS

Yearling Books
celebrates its
25 years—
and salutes
Reading Is
Fundamental®
on its 25th
anniversary.